The Paper Heart of Jack Leatherby

Second Edition

This Edition Published by HardtHouse

www.hardthouse.com

No one ever told me that
grief felt so like fear.
C. S. Lewis

Prologue

The sun was shining down brightly enough that the world was tinted with its glorious yellow glow. It was perfect picnic weather. Spring in England was my favourite time of the year. The sky was a happy blue; just the way it should be for her birthday. It was almost as if the world was giving her a present. I nibbled on one of the sandwiches that I had made for lunch, as I sat across from her. I could barely believe today was her 77th birthday. Where had the time gone?

I could hear the ducks quacking on the lake, just a few hundred feet behind us. If I twisted my stiff back, I could see them bobbing up and down on the water. I wanted to go down and feed them some of my sandwich, but I doubted that I would be able to walk down the slope that led to the lake without falling over. My old body was frailer than a piece of tissue paper, these days. In my mind, I was still nineteen years old. In my mirror, I was seventy-eight. I found it so strange that the man that was reflected back to me was wrinkled, with wispy tufts of white hair on a liver-spotted head. The man I knew was still just a boy inside.

Every so often, when I would allow my mind to wander, my body fills with lust for life, and I think of all the things I would still yet like to do. I could climb Mount Everest, or travel through Egypt to see the pyramids. All I need to do is go. But then, when it takes me longer than it should to get out of my chair, my heartbeat slows and I realise that I'm old now. I'll never get the chance to do those things. My back is hunched, and my eyes are weak. My hands are crooked, and my legs are slow. I've used up my time. I won't get it back. Then I remember my Gracie, and the love I have for her, and I realise it has been a life well spent. Isn't that the point?

Men can live adventurous lives, but feel empty when their time comes, if they've passed up love for the chance at power or money or fame. To be loved is life's greatest adventure - and I was fortunate enough to take part.

The wind blew across my face, cooling me from the warmth of the sun. "I told you today would be perfect," I said confidently. "That weatherman I like said so, and he's never wrong." I reached forward and plucked the packet of balloons from my bag, picking out three - one yellow, one white, and one green. It took a great deal more effort than I remembered to inflate them, and my wide fingers got stuck as I tried to tie the ends.

"Argh," I exclaimed in a quiet huff, so she wouldn't hear me. Things used to be so much easier.

I wrapped some string around the half blown up balloons and tied them to the picnic basket, so they wouldn't fly away. They flopped against the ground and writhed in the wind like dying snakes. I should have thought of using helium.

I spread out some more of the picnic food on the blue and white rug in front of her and placed the small gift, wrapped in silver and tied with a gold ribbon, right in the centre. She wasn't really one for gifts, but I had put a lot of effort into this one. I was worried that it might be the last birthday gift I would ever give her, so it had to be truly special. I was getting older and the doctor told me there was something wrong with me, but I didn't pay much attention to the details.

His message was clear; time was running out. Quickly.

I straightened the bow on the gift and hoped she would like it. She never had much of a desire for things. Her only hunger was for experiences, for life.

And what a life it had been.

Chapter One
December 31st, 1957

It began like any other great love story. Our eyes met across a crowded room; she was the honoured guest and I was the helping hand. She shouldn't have looked at me twice, and she wouldn't have if her parents had had any say in the matter.

It was New Year's Eve, 1957 and Grace was seventeen years old. She wore a light blue dress to the New Year's Eve Party thrown by her mother and father – a party that had been the talk of the town for months. I had been employed to serve drinks all evening – a job that hardly paid enough to be worth mentioning.

Her hair was loose around her shoulders, torn free from its tight confines the moment her mother had left the room, and she wore no makeup. She was the most beautiful woman in the room.

She smiled at me as she walked past, but I couldn't make myself respond. I was frozen where I stood, every ounce of a young man's invincibility abruptly gone. Suddenly I was vulnerable. Exposed. I knew there was no chance she would look my way again – that second, that smile, was all I was ever going to get. A fluke. A small hiccup in the smooth ebb and flow of the river of the universe.

But I was wrong.

She waltzed up to me not an hour later and asked me to dance.

"I c-can't," I stuttered back. "I'm working. We aren't supposed to mix with the guests."

Her lower lip jutted out as she took in my words, disappointment lining her face. Then she nodded solemnly and took the silver tray straight from my hands. She plopped it down on a nearby table, took my arm and led me out of the room.

She stopped in the courtyard and released me.

"I'm Grace," she said, holding out her hand for me to shake.

I stared at her, dumbfounded, until I found my voice. "Jack." I shook her hand and suddenly a smile as bright as the stars in the night sky lit up her face.

I had never seen anything more beautiful.

"Now we're friends," she said. Her voice was like liquid velvet. "And friends get to dance with each other. Haven't you heard?"

I knew in that moment that I was going to fall in love with her. It was only a matter of time.

She waited for me to take her in my arms, the softest smile on her face, and as soon as she placed her hand in mine, I was ruined.

People spend their entire lives looking for someone to love. But they spend an eternity hoping to be loved in return. Once love - a binding, reciprocated, passionate love - is found, it is never truly lost. Even if unforeseen events spiral out of control and human nature searches for another to blame, seeking to wound the soul closest to them, causing that love to fracture and become misplaced, it is always there. It lingers in the background of the mind, haunting every dream and aspiration. It remains in every kiss shared with another, every plan for a separated future, tainting their vision with the grey cloak of loss.

I could never look at another the same way, from that second onwards. If we were to be separated, any love I gave to another would be second best; just a leftover portion of something that should never have been divided.

She rested her head on my shoulder, and we danced to the music flowing from the ballroom of her parents' house. The earth continued to spin, strangers carried on their business and nothing of any great circumstance occurred to mark this moment. The world carried on, oblivious to the life-changing event taking place.

"Jack," she said to me, her head still against my chest as we swayed to the piano. "What do you think you would do if you could go anywhere in the world?"

I had never really thought about it. I could never imagine having the money to do anything of any value. "I don't know. I suppose I would..." I paused, really thinking through my answer. "I...I would see the world. Not the way the tourists see it, just following guidebooks and the road most travelled, but the truth, the essence of the city. I would find its soul and take pictures of it all."

She tilted her face to see mine. "You would?"

"I think so." I barely managed to reply. It didn't matter. I would never get the chance.

She smiled softly and stared at me with such intensity that I became lost in the depth of her brown eyes, the softness of her face.

"That's a good plan." She sighed, looking away as if saddened. I twirled her around until she faced me again.

"And you?" I asked. My heart was suddenly pounding, racing inside my chest.

She hesitated before sucking in a deep breath. "I want to travel. I want to see and touch and taste and hear everything the world has to offer. I don't want to be stuck in this place, masquerading as the perfect daughter and someday the perfect housewife. I couldn't care less about parties or my social status or even the size of the house I live in. I just want to be...free. I just want to live."

And that was it. I was in love. My heart vanished from my chest. It was hers.

Grace took a chance on a nobody. What she saw in me, I had no clue. Every moment I spent with her broadened my perspective on life. In the first month of our young love, she taught me more about life than I had ever learned in the nineteen years I'd been alive. As she took the time to discover me, I found that I was discovering myself, for the very first time.

Before Grace came into my life, I was only someone's son. Someone's employee. Someone's burden. I had never had the chance to just be *someone*.

A person who could love, live, learn, create, enjoy.

I had never believed that such things could be mine. Grace changed the colour of my sky. She opened my eyes to the dawn of a new day.

I worked like a dog when I wasn't with her. I knew she had no desire for fancy things, jewelry or expensive gifts, but all the same, I wanted to give that to her, and more. I wanted to take her around the world, show her England, France, Italy, everywhere I could. I wanted to be the one who would share her dream.

All that cost money. A lot of money. I worked longer hours at the garage I ran, doubling as manager and mechanic, and served drinks at every fancy party in town. Of course, my Gracie and her family were invited to all those parties, so I spent most of the time dancing with her in the courtyard, like we were the only two people alive.

She told me all about the books she had read, how the written word captivated her heart and her mind. There was so much passion in her voice, like the fate of the world was tied within the words of strangers. I established a deep love for reading because of her zest for well told stories.

"I just love the poetry in his words!" she sighed as we walked down the street in late January. "Have you ever heard someone speak with such imagination colouring their words?"

I shook my head.

"This J.R.R Tolkien is a literary genius! The way he describes everything is like...I don't know. I've never experienced it before. When I finished reading The Hobbit, I turned right back to the front page and started again."

"Why? You already know what happens." I gripped her hand in mine and let it sway back and forth like we were just two kids. In so many ways we were.

She turned to walk in front of me, still facing me and her fingers still laced between mine. "Because now I can appreciate its melody."

She stopped and looked at the ground, contemplating something far beyond the reaches of my mind. I took a deep breath, calming the fluttering butterflies that whirled around in my stomach. She didn't notice my hesitation, as absorbed as she was in her own thoughts. So, I bent my head down and kissed her.

She was surprised at first, having never been kissed before, but then her lips softened under mine and I pulled her closer to me. We were sure to be the victims of disappointed glares from passers-by and the tut-tuts of older women who would declare that this *would never happen in my day*. But we didn't notice. Or we didn't care enough to see.

Chapter Two

The sun was deepening in the sky one afternoon as I walked home from spending time with Grace. It was still hot, the air thick and dusty. My shirt clung to my back and my hair stuck to my forehead.

I walked up the driveway and opened the door. It crashed closed behind me and I bit my lower lip, hoping to avoid a belt across the head for slamming the door. However, my father was passed out on the lounge, a bottle of bourbon balanced precariously on the cushion, and as I walked past him to my room to change clothes, I shook my head in disgust.

Since my mother died, four years earlier, this was a daily occurrence, his ever-present state of being. He used to run the garage that we owned, but I had had to take over – the finance, wages, stock, everything. All because my father couldn't string two words together unless they were *Jack* and *Daniels*.

I'd had to drop out of school just before I turned fifteen to work full time and take care of my younger brother, Frankie.

He was fourteen now. Just young enough to think he was all grown up and just old enough to know he wasn't.

Opening my cupboard, I scanned through the nine or ten shirts I owned, looking for one of the work shirts. My searching fingers found one, fresh from the load of laundry I had done yesterday.

I looked at myself in the mirror on my cupboard and tried to straighten out my floppy dark blonde hair. It was no use. I tilted my head to the side and stared back at the blue eyes in front of me.

I had a tense jaw and smooth skin, save the long scar that lined the right side of my jawbone. I traced the tip of my finger along the risen, pale ridge. It had been there so long I couldn't even remember how I got it anymore.

I turned away from the face in the mirror and stumbled into the side of my small single bed. I grumbled something incomprehensible and left the room in search of my brother. My father's feet hung off the edge of the lounge chair and I kicked them as I passed.

"Get up, Dad. It's only three thirty in the afternoon." He barely stirred. I pulled the bottle free from his hands and tipped the liquid that remained out the window. He'd never know.

"Frankie?" I called, not bothering to keep my voice low out of respect for the sleeping member of the house. "Frankie, where are you?"

I found him in his room, staring at her picture, just like he always did.

I sighed. It ripped my heart out.

"She was really pretty, wasn't she?" Frankie said, wiping tears from his eyes.

"She sure was."

I dropped down on the edge of his bed and we sat there in silence, gazing at the old, deteriorating photo of our mother.

Its edges were ripped and torn, and the face was crinkled. Every day it faded a little more.

"I wish we had more photos of her," Frankie sighed, leaning into my shoulder.

"Yeah, I do too." My father had taken to drinking enough alcohol to knock out an entire football team one evening and had decided that he didn't want any more reminders of her. He lit a fire and sent her photos up in flames.

Frankie was only ten at the time, so all he could do was stand in the corner and cry, while the last tangible evidence of his mother's existence shriveled and burned in front of him. At fifteen, I was a little braver. I wrestled my father to the ground and prised a photo out of his hands before he punched me right in the eye and told me to get the hell out of his house.

He had never seemed smaller in my eyes than in that moment.

I had taken Frankie by the arm, grabbed the blanket off my bed and left. We slept on the train station bridge that night, freezing and uncomfortable. When the sun rose, we got up and I took him back home. There was nowhere else to go. Besides, I knew that our useless excuse for a father would have been too drunk to even remember what had happened.

"Come on, Frankie. You can't keep doing this to yourself. Put the photo down and come and help me in the shop. It'll keep your mind off things. Dallas has had to work an extra half hour as it is, and you know we can't afford it." I laughed, trying to lighten the mood.

He sighed and slipped the photo under his pillow. I wrapped my arm around his shoulders and led him out to the shop next door to our little house.

"Hey Dallas, we made it," I said, sliding open the stiff door.

"'Bout time!" I heard Dallas call from somewhere underneath the counter. "I was 'sposed to finish at three, Jackie."

Dallas was an old friend of the family. My father had hired him the day the shop opened, twelve years ago, and he was as loyal as he was big. Bald headed, wide chested and incredibly tall, Dallas was a gentle giant, and no one knew more about how to fix stubborn old cars than he did. He was a handy man to have working at our garage as we were the town's only mechanics.

"I know, I know. Sorry." I said, as he popped back up from behind the counter with a nail in his hand.

"I found it," he said, grinning at me gleefully over the nail. "Thing thought it could get away. Right. I'm out of here. See you boys tomorrow."

Dallas shook my hand and messed up Frankie's hair until it was covering his eyes.

"Thanks for staying," I called after him as he walked out the door. He waved his hand half-heartedly in response, as if to say, *"Don't worry. It's on the house."*

I appreciated his help. He and Dad had been close, but when my mother died, and he took to drinking, he pushed Dallas away. But Dallas stayed on at the shop and took care of Frankie and me whenever and however he could. It was Dallas who taught me how to run this place and how to fix the cantankerous vehicles that had often had me stumped.

The rest of the afternoon was spent the way it usually was – in the sweltering heat, stuck underneath cars trying to fix whatever problem they had and making sure Frankie didn't get pushed around by some skint customer who didn't want to pay his bill.

When I closed the shop that day, I felt the bone crushing weight of exhaustion cripple me. I was dragging the stubborn door forward, inch by inch, trying to lock it, when I saw her. She stood there staring at me with her big brown eyes, and I was amazed, all over again, that she cared for me.

I must have looked a mess. My jeans were smeared with grease, my shirt stained with the colour of sweat and hard labour. Black oil stained large chunks of my hair and my hands were rough and filthy.

She didn't seem to care.

She walked up to me and took my hands in hers, without noticing the coarse blisters or roughness.

"Hi," she said, smiling up at me.

"What are you doing here? It's five-thirty. Don't your parents usually crack up if you're late for dinner?"

"I'm on my way home now. I just finished with helping to teach the Cameron kids how to read."

"Oh, really?" I bent down and kissed her forehead.

"Yes," she laughed, pushing me away. "I'm a working-class girl now. The job pays just as badly as yours."

"No," I shook my head. "I'm not sure if that's possible." I chuckled and leant forwards to kiss her cheek.

She stiffened, suddenly looking angry.

"Gracie?" I raised my hand to tuck a wayward strand of her dark hair out of her face. "What is it?"

"It just makes me so mad," she said, crossing her arms.

"What does?" I asked, as her bottom lip jutted out the way it always did when she was upset, or deep in thought.

"You work so hard, and you get almost nothing in return. How is that fair? You're looking after your brother and the shop and your father. Plus, you work at every ridiculous party these pompous people plan in this stupid town. Then you spend every spare second you get with me. I'm so selfish. You never get to take care of yourself." Her voice broke as she spoke, and my heart thudded violently in my chest. I couldn't help but smile, though I fought against it.

"If spending time with you makes you selfish, then I don't mind at all. Please, be more selfish in the future, won't you?" I chuckled, trying to ease her mind.

"I'm not kidding, Jack. You deserve more." She looked to the ground and I could tell she was chastising herself in her mind.

"The only thing I want - the only thing that makes all of this," I gestured to the petrol pumps in front of us, "worth it - is knowing that I get you. You don't understand, Grace, spending time with you is me taking care of myself.

You make me want to be a better man. Sure, I got some tough cards dealt to me, but I also got some pretty good ones." I lifted her chin with my hand so that she could see the truth in my eyes.

We had only been seeing each other for two months, and I had loved her from the very first night, but I hadn't been able to tell her. Fear always crippled me, refusing to let the words escape my lips, though I knew I was being ridiculous. No one knew better than I did that life is short - you must seize every day. Well, this was a day that I was going to grab with both hands.

My pounding heart slowed and suddenly I felt completely serene. My fear dissipated, and my mind was clear. "Grace, I love you." The words came out clear and strong, and there was no doubt in my voice.

With her face still in my hand, I watched as the anger and frustration fell from her features. Her brows smoothed, and her jaw relaxed.

Suddenly her lips were on mine and she was kissing me furiously. She paused for a breath and crushed herself against me, wrapping her arms tightly around my neck. Then she whispered five words that forever changed my life. "I love you too, Jack."

Chapter Three

"You're acting ridiculous!" I shouted at her.

"And you're acting like an ignorant hick!" she screamed back.

"You think you're so entitled! You act like you don't care about money, but you do!"

"How dare you?" she screeched. "I have never made you feel like you don't give me enough! I can take care of myself!"

"Yeah, I know. You're so good at it that you don't let me do anything for you! You can't possibly accept any help from me!"

Our voices were echoing off the windows as we sat in the car screaming at each other. It was a rare occurrence for us to fight, but when we did, it was always at the top of our lungs.

"That's because I don't need any! When I need help, I'll ask for it! But what about you? You're so miserable sometimes!"

"I'm so sorry that I get tired from having to work twenty-four hours a day, look after my brother, and try to wake my drunk of a father out of his stupor. Please forgive me for not plastering a smile on my face when I get to see you!"

"Oh, you're such a jerk!"

"And you're a spoilt little girl! You won't even tell your parents about me! Sorry Grace, but that doesn't exactly make me feel really secure in our relationship!"

"Ugh," she scoffed. "I told you already, I don't need their permission and they won't understand anyway! You haven't told your father either!"

"That's because he's never conscious!"

"Oh, just go away!"

"You're in my car! You go away!"

She huffed out an angry breath and glared at me with fire in her eyes. "Fine," she snarled.

She got out of the car and slammed the door behind her, strutting off into the street.

I watched her stomp away and slammed my hands against the steering wheel, groaning with regret. Opening the car door, I got out without bothering to close it behind me.

I ran after her and scooped her up in my arms.

"Hey!" she yelled, slapping my chest. "Let go! Put me down!"

I trudged back to the car with her squirming in my arms and dropped her down on the passenger seat.

I leaned forward and kissed her, cutting off the complaint she was about to voice. I pulled back and sighed. "Want to go for a drive around the beaches?" I asked.

She smiled demurely and nodded, tucking in her legs. I closed the door behind her and shook my head, chuckling as I walked around to the driver's side. I would lose a thousand arguments if I had to. I never wanted to be the man who would let the woman he loved walk away. I would always go after her.

I had heard it said on many occasions that life is made up of moments. Moments that stun you, amaze you, break you, take your breath away and set your heart on fire. It seemed to me, that once Grace entered my life, I had more of these moments to make up my life's journey than I ever had before.

My parents had been the ones who defined me for so many years. The loss of my mother created in me a profound insecurity about my time here on earth. She vanished from my life, taken against her will. She was supposed to have been a constant pillar that supported me through the rough and tumultuous seas of time. Instead I was left to sail an ocean alone. Something had gone wrong in the universe. It wasn't meant to happen this way.

That one moment, when the doctor said there was nothing he could do, shaped our lives and changed our course forever. I was thrown into the life of a father at fifteen years of age. My childhood was stolen from me, along with my mother's warm smile and comforting presence. Gone were the days of adolescence, where my biggest decision during the day was, 'Do I do my chores now, or after I play football with the neighbours?'

The days of overdue bills, grocery shopping and working my fingers to the bone had arrived.

As my father slipped deeper and deeper into depression, he found his comfort in alcohol and left us floundering. The first time the bottle touched his lips, I became an adult, thrust forward in time.

I had found my identity in my loss. I pieced myself together, using the only materials available to me – crippling pain, bone-crunching anger, loyalty to my brother, and determination to survive after death had robbed me. I had an image in my mind of the man that I had to be, and when I continually failed to become him, it only served to stoop my shoulders and suffocate me, sucking the air from my lungs until I was drowning in mire of my failure.

Then Grace waltzed into my world and showed me what was real and what it meant to be alive. Her passion for life taught me that each day was an opportunity for great and extraordinary things to happen.

Slowly I peeled back the shell I had cocooned myself in and I was left with someone I didn't know or recognise but was beginning to love.

It was my firm belief that everyone was allotted only so much time during which they can blame someone else for who they were and how they acted. I had used up all that time. Suddenly I felt naked, exposed, left stranded in the middle of a wide-open field as I fought to navigate through the world in my new skin.

I couldn't blame my father for forcing me to become the man of the house; I couldn't blame death for taking my mother long before her time; I couldn't blame my brother for needing me or life for dealing me a mountain of anguish. But the hardest thing I had to face was that I could no longer hide behind it all. Once I understood the reasons behind my pain, they became excuses for not having to live my own life. I had to choose - life or servitude to old battle scars.

I had nothing to blame and no one to take responsibility. I was alone in the most peculiar way. It terrified and excited me, all at the same time.

It was in March that year that my newfound revelations were put to the test. How would this new man, that I was still getting to know, react to pain? Would he lash out in search of someone to take the fall?

I closed the garage early on the afternoon that everything changed. The heat was exhausting, and no one had come for petrol for the last hour and a half. I yanked the door closed and locked it behind me, plans to surprise Grace forming in my mind.

"Excuse me, are you Robert Leatherby?" A voice from behind me spoke in a businesslike tone.

I turned to see a man wearing a fedora and a deep blue suit. He stood in front of me, his arms folded tightly across his chest. Beside him stood a much shorter woman, her hair pulled tightly out of her face, making her expression severe.

"No, I'm his son, Jack Leatherby. Who are you?" I asked, matching his stance.

We had had our fair share of obnoxious visitors who continued to stick their nose where it didn't belong. Each face blurred into the next as they made their threats about taking the house, or closing the garage, due to our struggle with meeting our bills. Lately, however, they were questioning our ability to look after Frankie.

Whoever these people were, they wouldn't be bringing good news and I didn't want anything to do with them.

"My name is Garret Lang, and this is Susan Keynes. We're here about the unsatisfactory living conditions of one..." he looked at his piece of paper, searching for a name, "...Franklin Leatherby."

"Come again?" I said, gritting my teeth. "What *unsatisfactory living conditions* are you talking about? There isn't anything unsatisfactory about it."

This Garret Lang irritated me immediately. The others had been politer, just making sure the house was clean and tidy and no knives were sticking out of the floorboards or anything. This man was getting straight to the point, normally a trait that I admired, but I couldn't help but feel an intense desire to punch him in the face.

"Calm down, young man. This is none of your concern. Just let us in and take us to your father."

"I don't know if that's something I really want to do, sir. Why don't you just leave?" I clenched my fists together angrily.

"I'm afraid we can't do that, son. Now, let us in the house." The man had a deep voice and an angry scowl.

There was nothing more I could do or say that would convince him to leave.

I turned around and stormed off towards the house, a quick pace flicking dust up with every step. I fervently wished each dust cloud would cake all over their freshly pressed clothes.

I led them around the garage and up the driveway to the house sitting at the back. When we reached the front door, I stopped and spun around to face them. "I'm going to ask you to wait here while I get my father. Then he can decide whether you do or do not come in."

"We have to come in, son. There's no way around it." Garret took off his hat and took a step forwards. I held out my hand, about a foot away from his chest. I was not going to let them push me around.

"All the same, I'll let him make that decision," I replied, fighting to keep my voice under control.

I slammed the door in their faces and stomped through the house. I didn't need to look for him – I knew where he would be. I arrived at the sitting room and found him sprawled out on the couch. I bent down and shook him aggressively. "Dad, wake up. There are some people here who want to talk to you about Frankie." My voice was urgent, quivering just enough to shake my words.

He grumbled something unintelligible in response.

"Dad!" I all but shouted at him.

Still nothing.

I stood up and kicked him, fair in his ribs. He spluttered awake and sat up, shouting at me. "What the hell are you doin'?"

"Dad, there are some Government people here to talk to you about Frankie's living conditions. Sober up so you can convince them he's fine."

There was a vacant expression on his face, before the words finally sunk in.

"Coffee, Jack. I need coffee."

I ran into the kitchen and made him up a steaming cup of the black brew, making it stronger than normal. I needed him sober. Quickly.

I heard him knocking things over and shuffling through drawers in his room, probably looking for something more appropriate than a singlet and shorts to wear.

"We're still waiting here, Jack," I heard the woman shout from the door.

Like I could forget.

"Just a minute," I snapped back, barely able to keep my voice even.

My father stumbled into the kitchen, tucking in his brown shirt. I handed him the cup and he slurped, making a face when he realised how strong it was.

"They're at the door," I said, ushering him forward.

I stayed in the kitchen, my feet frozen to the floor. I fought against the questions circling my mind. Why were they here? Were they going to

take my brother away?

"How can I help you?" I heard my father slur.

I rolled my eyes. Very convincing.

"Sir, we'd like to come inside and speak to you for a moment, if that's alright," Garret said. His voice was sharp, like needles in my ears.

"Uh, sure. We have nothing to hide."

I almost scoffed. What about the liquor collection in his cupboard? The empty bottles in the bin? The bourbon stains on the lounge chair?

Just then my eyes fell on a half empty bottle of scotch, balanced precariously on the bench. I bounded over to it and threw it in the cupboard below the sink, just as they walked into the kitchen.

"What's this about?" he asked as Garret and Susan took a seat at the kitchen table.

"Mr. Leatherby, we've received some interesting complaints about Franklin's living conditions. We think it may be in his best interest that he be placed in foster care for the foreseeable future."

There was dead silence.

The seconds passed with agonizing intensity. I couldn't handle it anymore and I exploded. "What? Just like that? What the hell do you mean he needs to be placed in foster care? You haven't even seen the house! Look – it's clean! The others have come and seen that! He's fine! How dare you think you can just walk in to my house and take my brother away!"

"Mr. Leatherby, I suggest that you rein in your son. We don't need to see the house. It's not the cleanliness we're concerned about. And, yes, I know the others have come. That's why we're here. We have received more than one complaint about this family situation and we are under instruction to take Franklin into foster care. Today. This is not up for negotiation."

"Hell, yeah, it's up for negotiation!" I shouted.

"Jack!" my father yelled, raising his hand to silence me. A look of shame and defeat flitted across his face. "It's over."

"No, it's not!" I couldn't believe he was willing to let these strangers take Frankie away, without fighting back. "It is not over! You can't take him!"

"As always," Susan spoke harshly, "our intention is to restore, not divide, so –"

"Really?" I cut her off. "Because so far all I'm seeing is division!"

She glared at me, her lips pursing.

"So," Garret took over as if I hadn't spoken at all. "I will be checking in via the telephone on a trimonthly basis to see if the issues that have been raised with us have been rectified. It is not our desire to see Franklin become a permanent member of the foster care system. He will be placed in another home until such a time that we deem it is safe for him to come home. We take foster care very seriously, Mr. Leatherby, and if conditions do not improve here, Franklin will remain in care until he reaches the legal age of twenty-one or is able to financially support himself."

My stomach rolled. Twenty-one. That was seven years away. If my father didn't quit drinking and straighten himself out, my brother was going to be in foster care until he was an adult. I felt tears sting my eyes.

I knew, beyond the shadow of a doubt, that if it came to giving up his son, or giving up his booze, Frankie was going to lose.

"Who the hell do you think you are?" I bellowed.

"Young man," Susan snarled. "Control yourself. Remember that you are only nineteen. You are not beyond the realms of foster care."

"But I can financially support myself!"

"Can you?" Susan smirked cruelly. "That's not what the reports say."

Garret appeared not to have heard the threats that had tried to silence me. "Where is your son now, Mr. Leatherby?" he asked, forcing a pleasant smile to his face.

"Uh," my father cleared his throat. "He's on his way home. He shouldn't be too much longer."

I felt anger and hatred bubble up inside of me, making a potent blend that was about to erupt. I had to get out of here. I picked up the ceramic coffee pot and I hurled it against the wall, a furious roar escaping my lips. It shattered into a million tiny pieces. Garret and Susan jumped at my sudden display, but didn't respond beyond exchanging knowing, smug glances with each other as if this act of pain cemented their unforgivable act. If they spoke, I didn't hear it. I was out of the room without a second glance.

I burst through the back door and into the suffocating heat. I couldn't breathe, couldn't think. I grabbed fistfuls of my hair and crumpled to the ground, my legs suddenly unable to support me. I couldn't leave, though I was desperate to. I wanted to run away, to leave this town forever, to bury myself in another world, but Frankie was going to be home any minute and, if I left, I wouldn't get to say goodbye.

I couldn't do that to him.

I felt sick with fury and disgust. How could my father let this happen? How could he sit there and be satisfied with the fact that they were going to take his son away from him?

"Argh!" I screamed, waving my hands around and punching the air. I wished the air could feel pain, so my punches wouldn't be useless. I wanted it to feel what I felt.

How could this be happening? My skin felt as hot as flames and my heart pounded in my chest so violently that I thought it was going to come to an abrupt and sudden halt, just out of pure exhaustion.

I flopped against the dry grass, heaving in deep breaths, suddenly weary and weak. There was absolutely nothing I could do. They were going to take away my brother and I was powerless to stop them.

I heard the front door open and knew that Frankie was home. I stood up and shook the grass from my body. It was going to kill me to walk back into that house, but I had to find the strength. I took one shaky step forward, followed by another and then another until I reached the back door.

Frankie was in the kitchen, talking to Garret and Susan. I stayed hidden behind the wall of the corridor, not yet brave enough to face the room.

"Dad?" I heard Frankie say in a weak voice.

He didn't respond.

"Dad!" I heard him say again, tears making his voice thick.

He still didn't respond.

My heart seized in my chest, breaking at the sound of his voice. I leant around the wall and looked at him. His lower lip trembled, and his face was red and puffy with tears. His chest rose up and down so fast that you could barely see the movement. He was staring at the ground, hands shoved in his pockets.

Our father was tapping his foot silently on the ground, pretending to examine his hands.

Suddenly, Frankie's head snapped up and he looked at me. I almost fell apart. It took all I had not to fall to pieces, right there and then.

I held out my hand to him and he ran, shoving past our father, straight into my arms.

I put my hand against his head and stared at the man I would never call Dad again. He met my gaze, shame etched into every line on his skin. I locked my jaw and hoped the fire in my eyes would burn him, right down to the pit of his stomach. I hoped the scars left behind would never heal.

I led Frankie from the room, into his bedroom where we had the grueling, heartbreaking task of packing his things.

We didn't speak for a few long minutes, before Frankie finally fell against his bed and sobbed.

Not this. Not *this*. I couldn't bare his pain. It tore at my limbs and stung my eyes. His pain was excruciating to me.

I put my hand on his head as he squashed his face deeper into his pillows. "Hey," I said, "Frankie, come on. It's going to be alright. Sit up."

I pulled him free of his pillow and let him bury his head in my chest.

"Frankie, I'm going to do everything I can to get you back home as soon as possible. This is just temporary. I...I promise I'll fight for you."

I knew the fight would be useless. There was nothing I could do.

"I don't understand. Everything's fine. Don't they see that? You take care of me just fine, Jack!" he said through sobs.

"I know, Frankie. I think that's the problem. It's not you, it's not me, it's him. Once he sorts himself out, you'll be back home, and things can go back to normal."

"Why can't they take him away instead? I don't want to leave you!"

I almost chuckled. If only they *would* take him away instead.

"I don't want you to leave either. But maybe it won't be so bad where you're going. Maybe they'll own a dog that you can play with or live nearby so we can still see each other."

"They don't." Frankie wiped his tears away with his sleeve.

"Oh, come on, you don't know for sure. They could live just down the road." I allowed myself to hope for a split second that maybe, just maybe, this was true.

"They don't. Garret already told me that they live six hours drive away."

I felt like the air was punched from my lungs. Six hours.

There really was nothing to say to that. I gently pried Frankie's arms apart and slipped myself out of his grasp. We spent the next hour packing his things, barely uttering a word to each other. What was there to say?

The muggy heat was lessening as we piled his belongings into the backseat of the car. It was time for him to leave. I wish I had known it would be my last day with my brother. If I had have known, I would have kept him home from school, walked with him, talked to him. Maybe I could have given him advice or bought him a gift or something. Not that anything I could do

would make a difference.

I bent to my knees, so I was closer to his height and hugged him goodbye.

He held out his hand for Robert to shake and didn't bother to look him in the eyes.

"I'll see you soon," I promised him as he squashed himself in between his bags in the back seat of the grey car.

He just nodded.

Garret tipped his hat as if he had done us a great service and Susan smiled, revealing a row of crooked teeth. They dropped themselves into the car and drove away, taking a little piece of me with them.

Suddenly, I had a gut-wrenching thought. I ran into the house and yanked the pillow from his bed. Sure enough, the photo of our mother was still there.

I sprinted back out, as fast as my legs could carry me, and ran down the driveway after them. I waved my arms in the air, screaming and shouting.

I prayed they would notice me. He needed this photo. He looked at it every day. He couldn't leave to a stranger's home without it.

For a few terrifying moments, I thought they weren't going to stop the car. I thought they were going to drive on and disappear out of my sight. But, finally, after I had run almost a quarter mile after them, they stopped.

Frankie opened his door as I approached the car, breathless. "You..." I said, sucking in deep breaths, "forgot your photo."

Frankie looked at me and tried to smile. It fell flat. "No, I didn't forget it. I left it for you. I thought you might be lonely without me, and you could talk to her, just like I do."

It felt as though someone had my throat in their hands and was squeezing the life out of me.

I bent down and hugged him, before I pulled back and put the photo on

his lap. "No," I said, smiling softly. "You keep it. Because I want it back soon, and that means we're going to have to see each other. Alright?"

He nodded, and I closed the car door, watching it vanish around the corner.

Chapter Four

I had never felt such a sense of emptiness. I had fought for Frankie since he was ten years old. I had kept him fed and healthy with a clean home to shelter him. I had made sure he was focused on his studies and passed all his subjects in school. I had comforted him when he cried and helped him to understand what had happened to the stable family unit that he used to know.

What was the use? They took him anyway. He was gone, and he wasn't coming back. Not until he was twenty-one years old. A man. A different person. One whom I wouldn't recognise.

The dust had not yet settled from our driveway that stretched parallel to the garage, and I felt as though a thousand days had already passed. I stared down the drive towards the road, completely numb.

Robert looked at me, but I refused to meet his gaze. He kicked his foot in the dirt, scuffing up little red clouds of dust, and cleared his throat. He knew better than to speak to me. He simply turned around and walked back inside the house.

I stood there, motionless in my grief, until the sun began to set, and the white clouds were painted with orange, pink and red. The heat of the day vanished from the atmosphere, leaving a cool breeze in its wake.

Before I was consciously aware of it, my feet were carrying me forwards, out of my driveway and down the street. I walked for days and months and years, all in the space of an hour. I was aging. By the time I reached her house, I felt like an old man. My hair should be grey and stringy, my back should be bent and my eyesight should be failing. But it wasn't. I was still just nineteen. No time had passed at all.

I wasn't sure how long I waited outside Grace's house. Her parents knew nothing of me and it would only cause her trouble if I knocked on the door of her enormous house.

Instead, I walked underneath a streetlamp, pacing back and forth, lost in my aching thoughts, until the night sky loomed far above me and the stars danced around the pale moon.

"Jack?"

I turned to see her standing behind me, her face weary with concern. The yellow dress she wore cascaded down past her knees and her hair fell in loose curls around her face, highlighted by the soft glow from the streetlamp. Just the sight of her eased the acidic burn in my chest.

She stepped towards me and I could hold it in no longer. I fell to my knees, my head in my hands, and wept. I didn't care if I looked like a fool. I trusted her with my pain. I was vulnerable to her in that moment, my soul bared for her to see just how broken it was.

She dropped by my side and wrapped me in her arms. I felt her warmth sooth my pain as she ran her fingers through my hair.

My tears would not ease. It was as though there was an endless supply, or a lifetime's worth of agony was escaping in this one moment. I rested my forehead on her shoulder and she pressed her palm against my tear stained cheek.

She didn't pester me with questions about what brought on my hysteria. She just let me cry, ruining her dress with my salty tears, emptying my hopelessness out onto the street.

Somewhere in the back of my mind, I couldn't help but realise how truly blessed I was to have found love. I had never believed what they said about love. I had never believed that it could change a man, or alter the way he viewed the world. It wasn't something phenomenal. It wasn't the beginning or the end of the world.

How truly naïve I had been.

I had never loved my Grace more than I had in that moment. I was a six foot three, grown man, balled up on the ground in the middle of the street, wedged into her comforting arms, crying like a baby. Yet, she never made me feel small or weak.

When my tears had finally run dry, she lifted my head, the tips of her fingers under my jaw. I fought against it, not wanting her to see my puffy, splotchy face, but she didn't give up until we were face to face. I kept my eyes closed.

"Open your eyes," she pleaded.

Begrudgingly, I opened them and stared into her eyes. Her face showed the signs of recent tears, and I knew she had shed her own along with me. She didn't appear at all disgusted by my pathetic appearance.

"I love you, Jack," she whispered. Then she leaned forward and kissed my forehead, pressing her head against mine.

She pulled back and traced her fingers along the lengthy scar on my jaw. She smiled softly, unappalled by the ugly ridge on my face.

I reached up my hand and laced her fingers between mine. Standing to my feet, I gently pulled her up with me. I wrapped my arms around her waist and felt the beats of her heart drum against my chest.

We stood there until the night grew cool, barely moving our feet. She rested her head into my shoulder and I listened to her soft breathing, content and peaceful.

Nothing had been solved, no wounds had been healed and Frankie was still going to be living six hours away from me, but somehow, it seemed as though I would be able to manage. I would be able to survive.

I kissed the top of her head. "I love you, Gracie."

She lifted her head from my chest and stood on her toes to reach up and kiss me. As our lips moved softly together, I knew I could face whatever tomorrow would bring, as long as she was by my side.

The sheeting rain began to pour, instantly heavy, drenching us in the warm torrent within seconds.

We didn't notice.

I held her close to me, more passion and adoration in the kiss than ever before. I cradled her face in my hands as the rain dripped down my neck and along my spine.

I could feel her begin to shiver, so I gently pushed her away with a breathless chuckle.

"You should go back inside," I said as I watched her teeth chatter. "You're cold."

"No," she said, tightening her grip around my neck and leaning her head on my chest. "I'm n-not c-cold."

I laughed. "Yes, you are, get inside. Go on, get out of here."

She pulled back and sighed, her blue lips pouting. "Okay," she grumbled through chattering teeth. She rose on her toes to kiss me one last time and turned on her heels, heading back for her house. She paused only a few feet away from me. "Are you going to be alright?"

I smiled weakly and nodded.

She stopped at her front door and waved goodbye, before disappearing inside her house.

I headed back down the street, the heavy rain still pounding against my back. I turned up my collar and listened to the splash of my boots in the water that covered the ground.

I was soaked through to the bone, but I didn't mind. I was cold, but it didn't bother me. My mind was too focused on how to get through the next seven years of my life. Things would never be the same again and I had to figure out how I was going to deal with this brand-new way of life.

I wondered if there was a limit to the pain one person could bear. When was enough going to be enough?

When I arrived home, I was surprised to see it was after nine thirty. I kicked off my boots at the door and pulled off my sopping socks so I could walk through the house without making a mess that I would just have to clean up later.

I walked past Frankie's room and stopped at the door. I couldn't face any more today. With a heavy heart, I pulled his door closed and walked to my room.

"Why the hell are you all wet?" a gruff voice asked, stopping me.

"I went for a walk and it started to rain." My voice was flat, monotone.

"You should have called me. I could have collected you."

I scoffed quietly. I didn't really feel like dying in a car crash tonight because Robert was drunk at the wheel. Besides, he and I both knew he hadn't driven in over three years.

"I was fine," I settled for replying.

"Look, Jack, I know you're angry about Frankie, and I am too, but there's nothing we can do about it now. We've got to stick together."

I scoffed louder. This time he heard me.

"Hey! Don't give me disrespect, son. I'm your father. Now, Frankie's gonna be fine in foster care. He'll be twenty-one before he knows it."

I clenched my fists. He wasn't even going to try giving up the booze.

Robert stood in front of me, swaying slightly on his feet. He hadn't shaved in days, so a carpet of hair covered his face. He wore a singlet that was stained with last night's dinner and reeked of bourbon. "Frankie's tough. But, like I said, I'm your father and I don't need your attitude. They took him and now we have to deal with it."

"Now you want to be my father? You haven't been my father since she died!" I knew better than to refer to her as anything other than *she* around him. "You didn't even fight for Frankie! You just let them take him! The worst part about it is that I expected you to fight for him. How stupid could I be? You don't even know him! Why would you care?"

"What could I have done?" he roared at me. His voice was loud and furious. "What did you want me to do, Jack? Huh? You want me to tackle them? Hold a gun to their heads and tell them to get lost? What good would that have done? They took him, and I'm real sorry about that, but you know what – that's life!"

"No! That's not life! That's your excuse! I've been building a life around here for us, a home - with food on the table and enough money to pay the mortgage. That's life. That's reality. But you know what, people go through hard times, and people lose their loved ones, and they don't fall apart! They get up and they keep living. They don't drink themselves into a grave and lose their son to foster -"

The punch that landed across the right side of my face cut me off from finishing my sentence. I staggered back, before I regained my composure. I lifted my hand to touch my cheek and felt soft, oozing blood drip down my split skin.

Suddenly I remembered where the long scar on my jaw had come from.

I nodded and let out a half-hearted laugh, unsurprised. I looked down at the glass of brown liquid in his hands. "I sure hope you didn't spill any there. That would be a real shame."

I turned around and walked to my room, leaving him to drown in the company of the only thing left in the world that he loved.

Chapter Five

I took the car, a rusty Willys Jeep Truck, without asking – Robert wouldn't notice anyway, and I didn't want to break the four-day silence.

I drove until I reached Grace's street. She was waiting for me, five doors down from where she lived, wearing a flowing white dress that reached to just below her knees. She had loosely pulled back her chestnut hair and was holding a little basket.

"Hey, I said I would bring the food," I laughed as she hopped into the passenger side.

She leant forward and kissed me gently. "I know, but we didn't discuss dessert. How good can a bonfire be without strawberries and chocolate brownies?"

"Of course. What was I thinking?" I chuckled, pulling out onto the road.

The beach was empty, thanks to the overcast weather. That suited us just fine. We wouldn't risk running into any friends of Grace's parents. She still hadn't found the courage to tell them about me.

I tried not to read anything into it.

I piled on the sticks and leaves until I was satisfied and lit the fire. I wasn't sure if this was exactly legal, but by this stage we were so far along the beach, I doubted anyone would see us.

The orange tongues of fire flickered to life and we sat down, watching it dance in front of us.

It never ceased to amaze me that we didn't have to speak to enjoy each other's company. Life is busy, distracting and loud. To sit in silence, basking in quiet companionship, was new to me. It was comfortable, natural.

I watched the world reflected in Grace's eyes as she alternated between watching the waves lap lazily against the shore and the fire devouring the bits of nature at its disposal.

"Have you heard from Frankie?" she asked, so quietly I could barely hear her.

"No," I sighed. "I wrote him a letter yesterday. I don't know when he'll get it."

"I can't believe what happened. It's so unfair."

"I know." I cleared my throat, forcing the rising lump away.

Gracie reached up and touched the healing slice on my cheek. "I...I don't even..." she paused and sucked in a few tense breaths. "Does it still hurt?"

"No," I lied. "It's fine. Don't worry." I took her hand in mine and kissed her palm. "It's not a big deal."

She scoffed and pulled her hand away. When I told her what happened, I had to convince her that arriving at my front door and 'giving him a taste of the dinner he dishes out' was not a good idea. She was ropable. She may have been little in stature, but she was tough. I didn't doubt that she could throw a good punch.

"I want to ask you something," she said after some time. I could tell from her tone that she had calmed down again and was on to another subject.

"Of course," I answered. "What is it?"

"Well, I'm turning eighteen in a few weeks."

"I know."

"My infuriating parents are throwing this ridiculous party. Obviously, I have to go, and I was thinking that it is going to be completely intolerable."

"You're probably right." I took a bite of a jam and turkey sandwich.

"But then I kept on thinking and I realised that it would be much more of an agreeable affair if..." she paused, as if gathering courage. "...if you came." She bit her bottom lip, waiting for my reaction.

I swallowed. "Gracie," I whined.

"Please?" she begged. "Please, please, please."

"Gracie, it's not that I don't want to spend your birthday with you, you know that. It's just that I'm not welcome in those circles. The only reason I'm ever even allowed within the gates is if I'm wearing an apron and holding a silver tray."

"But I'm inviting you. I'll put your invitation in the pile – that way you'll even have the obnoxious little piece of paper that goes hand in hand with these insufferable occasions."

"Grace, your parents don't even know about us. There will probably be a dozen guys there, just waiting for a chance to prove themselves to you. If I'm there beating them away with a stick, your parents are sure to notice and then have me thrown out."

She began to laugh and slapped my arm. "Stop it! You make it sound like a meat market."

"Well," I said, chuckling. "Can you blame them? Look at you," I said, kissing her cheeks. "You're perfect."

"Yeah, yeah," she mumbled. "But won't you even consider it? As a gift to me?"

Her eyes were pleading, and her lower lip jutted out.

I groaned. "Oh, fine."

"Yay!" she cheered, wrapping her arms around my neck. "Thank you, thank you, thank you."

It was my turn now. "Yeah, yeah."

Grace pulled away and stood up. "Isn't it beautiful?" she sighed, twirling around, finding incomprehensible joy in the simple act of being. I heard thunder rumble and saw lightning strike behind her. The contrast of this gentle creature against a violent storm far off at sea was breathtaking.

I pulled out my camera, my most treasured possession, and photographed her swirling around, smiling and laughing. After some time, she flopped down on the sand and laughed, exhausted.

I had taken some beautiful photos.

"Jack!" I heard my voice called out from a long way away. I looked up and saw someone running down the beach, arms flailing wildly. "Jack!"

"What's going on?" Grace asked.

"I don't know." I stood up and began jogging towards the man. As I got closer, I could see it was my neighbour.

"James, what's wrong?" I asked, suddenly panicked.

"It's the garage," he said, puffing and resting his hands on his knees. "I went out looking for you. I saw your Jeep parked up on the road and came down to find you."

"What's happened to the garage, James?" I asked.

"There's been a fire. Come on!" He turned and ran.

I looked over at Grace and followed after him.

Chapter Six

A large portion of the garage was charred and smoking, embers still flickering with the threat of destruction. The fire had been put out and I stood motionless in front of the Jeep, my arms wrapped across my chest. Grace was speaking to a fireman a few feet away, trying to understand what had happened, but I couldn't move.

I knew that I should be feeling something. Horror? Pain? Fear? But I wasn't. I felt nothing. I stood staring at it all with a hollow feeling in the pit of my stomach.

Why wasn't I angry? Why wasn't I relieved that it hadn't been worse? I was an empty shell, staring at the mess as if it had nothing at all to do with me. I turned my head and looked over at my Gracie, who was deep in conversation with the very distracted fireman. He was trying to get away from her and carry on his duties, but she wouldn't let him go. I smirked as she stomped her foot and crossed her arms. She went to war for the people she loved, and I felt honoured to be included in that small group of people.

Robert was sitting on the edge of the gutter, his head in his hands. He looked a man twice his age. I tried to recall a time when his company was something that I loved, something that I craved. But as the years flicked past me in the cinema of my mind, the only prominent face I saw was my mother's – Lucy Jane.

She had been the one who would tell us that we were loved. She had cared for us, fought for us and taught us how to be people who deserved their space on earth. She was a graceful warrior and she, too, would go to war for the ones she loved.

Robert was just a smudged image in my many memories; it seemed his love was only for my mother. I supposed that I owed him gratitude for that, as his adoration for her could never be called into dispute. I guessed it didn't matter so much if he didn't love us, if my mother was well taken care of until her last days.

Unfortunately, Frankie was never quite as good at lying to himself, as I was. He didn't understand. He still craved his father's love, when I had convinced myself that I no longer needed it. I had never been able to be a good enough replacement for him.

I sighed and walked over to where Robert sat, looking depleted and alone. Sitting down beside him, I felt little droplets of light rain land on my skin.

Ironic.

"I can't...I don't even know how it happened. I...I was just..." Robert trailed off and shook his head from side to side.

I took a deep breath. I was struck with the sudden realisation that this was a defining moment in my life. How would this new man that I had become react to this situation? To the man who was responsible?

I looked over to Grace, who had her hand on the fireman's arm, refusing to let him go, and decided that I wanted to be the man that she deserved.

I put my hand on Robert's back. He looked at me, startled, and I pressed my lips into a thin line before speaking. "It's okay."

His eyes brimmed with tears he would never shed, and he nodded weakly.

I heard Grace's footsteps behind me. I stood up and met her halfway.

"He says that we should all be grateful that there wasn't more damage. Apparently, your father was drinking in the shop and... I don't know. They're not sure yet," she sighed, frustrated.

"It's okay. It'll be alright."

"How can you say that? It's..." she turned and looked at the charred remains, "...horrible. I feel awful for you."

I smiled at her worried face and kissed her forehead. "Don't. It's fine."

She pulled back and looked at me as if I were a great mystery, unsolvable and confusing.

"What?" I asked. "Something on my face?"

"No," she said, shaking her head. "It's just...you look fine. If this was my place, I'd be a wreck, and you're...not."

"I know. It's got to mean something tragic, doesn't it? I don't know. I just... don't feel anything. I guess it's because it's not a surprise. I'm disappointed that this has happened I suppose, but it's fixable, and it was only a matter of time, really."

"No, it wasn't. This shouldn't have happened. He shouldn't have been... ugh!"

"But he was," I said, tucking a rebellious strand of her hair behind her ear. "And it did. It's just a building. I'll fix it. Eventually. At least there's still enough left untouched that we can stay open and I can still pay the bills."

I surveyed the damage again and then took another look at the downcast man in the gutter, muttering to himself and twirling his wedding band around his finger. He was so broken. So lost. I almost felt sorry for him. I would have, too, if his despair wasn't dealt from his own hand.

The same hand he had been playing for far too many years.

Chapter Seven

Parties were the main social outlet for the aristocrats in my town. The elaborate affairs would serve to accentuate the deep canyon that separated the rich from the poor with a flurry of frilly dresses and coat tails.

Usually, I would serve the attendees with drinks all evening, ensuring the majority were just tipsy enough to think they were having a good time among the stuffy conversation and horrible finger food.

Tonight, however, was an exception. It was April 9th – Grace's eighteenth birthday. I was dreading the evening, but I was desperate to not let her see it.

I was wearing my best suit, but I had a daunting feeling that my best was still nowhere near good enough. I was well aware that this was something that seeped into more than just my wardrobe.

I was not educated enough to be able to carry on meaningful conversations about art or war or philosophy, and I knew nothing of life in their eyes. Grace's parents, Sylvia and Louis, were wealthy. Louis had come from a long line of prominent lawyers, and Sylvia had wormed her way into a life of luxury, trading tin cups for silverware. I had heard through the constant stream of town gossip that they were tough to please and had learned that for myself when I served drinks at their party, the first night I met Grace.

To say I was nervous would be an understatement.

I parked my rusty car at the very end of their street, so it would not draw attention, and walked down the sidewalk. I regarded the guests as they poured from the many vehicles, dressed in expensive and flamboyant outfits and holding beautifully wrapped boxes. No doubt they would contain thoughtless, yet costly gifts.

Suddenly the small gift tucked into my coat pocket felt extraordinarily heavy. I made a mental note to give it to her in private. There was no way I was going to put the tiny rectangle on her gift table.

I stopped at the door and handed the man my invitation. He looked at me skeptically, before pursing his lips and allowing me inside.

The house was decorated lavishly with ribbons of yellow winding intricately through the hallways and into the ballroom.

I almost rolled my eyes. There was barely anyone present that Grace would ever care to speak to. I could instantly see that this was her mother's party, not hers.

My eyes followed her as she walked up to an elderly woman and gently kissed her cheeks. Her smile was genuine and there was light in her eyes. The way Grace's mother supported the woman's hand told me the she was likely to be Grace's grandmother.

I stood alone near the hallway for a long while, just watching her laugh and delight in her frail looking relative. Grace wore her long hair down, as she usually did, letting it softly curl past her shoulders. Her floor length dress was black and flowed down her frame, with a swooping neckline and wide straps. She looked incredible.

When she looked up and saw me, a smile lit up her face and I had to stop myself from literally going weak at the knees.

She floated through the crowd and stopped in front of me. "Well?" she asked, twirling around. "What do you think?"

"You look beautiful," I said softly.

She bit her lower lip and sighed. "It's horrible, isn't it?" She gestured to the room.

"No," I said, trying to be uplifting. "It's...very, uh, tasteful. Elegant."

"Yeah," she said sarcastically. "*It's positively wonderful, Grace. You should be delighted we're going to so much trouble for you.*" Her imitation of her mother was spot on. I chuckled hysterically. "I'm really glad you came, though, Jack. Thank you."

I just smiled before whispering, "Incoming."

She rolled her eyes and turned around. "Hello, Mother. Are you having a nice time?"

"Yes, dear," Sylvia replied. She was a tall, lovely woman with exceptional taste. She had learned how to be the ultimate aristocrat's aristocrat. She regarded me coolly. "Grace, darling, you're ignoring the rest of your guests. Come along."

Grace turned back to me. "If you'll excuse me, Jack, I'm being a terrible hostess and I have to go and right my wrongs."

I did my best to refrain from laughing.

Sylvia tugged on her arm and led her through the room, whispering in her ear things I was sure I didn't want to hear.

As soon as Sylvia was busy talking to a guest, Grace found me again and pulled me out into the courtyard.

"Remember the first time we danced?" she asked when we stepped out into the cool air.

Yeah, like I could forget. "I do," I answered.

She smiled and sat down on the bench.

"Happy birthday," I said, pulling out her gift from my jacket.

She looked up at me and her face crumpled. "What?" she sighed. "Why are you getting me a gift?"

"Well, because it's customary that when one has a birthday, one receives gifts. Plus, I love you and I wanted to get you something."

"Jack, I've got you - that's all I want. Let *me* spoil *you*. I don't want you spending money on me."

"Just take it and stop being such a pain," I said teasingly, extending my hand.

Her bottom lip jutted out the way it always did, and she reluctantly took the gift from my hand.

I held my breath. Would she like it? *Please, please, please.*

She gasped, and her lips fell apart. She traced her fingers around the intricately carved frame I had made. Inside was a photo of her that I had taken when we were at the beach, the day of the fire at the garage.

She was spinning, her arms out from her side, and her hair was blowing in the breeze. Just behind her was a bolt of lightning, slapping the sea with incredible force.

She looked up at me with tears in her eyes.

"I know it's not very much, but I thought that..." I trailed off.

"Thank you," she breathed.

"Grace!" Sylvia called loudly. "Grace, darling, where are you?"

Grace bit her lip and I sighed. Leave it to Sylvia to ruin the moment. "Let's go inside. Your mother will have a fit if you're found with me again."

She scoffed. "Coming, Mother," she trilled.

I followed her inside and fell into the crowd, disappearing into a sea of identical suits. I kept my eyes on Grace as she found her mother and was dragged onto the small stage that lined the front wall. The band had moved back, leaving a large space for the presenters of the speech I presumed was coming.

Sylvia wore an olive-green dress that reached to her knees. Her hair was expertly twirled and pinned until it looked just so. She smiled demurely at her audience as she stepped up on stage with Grace in tow.

She wasn't a bad mother, of this I was sure. She loved Grace and wanted only the very best for her. She had plans for her future, blueprints on exactly how her daughter's life should look. The problem was that Grace didn't want any of it. She wasn't interested in the life of a socialite, or getting into the right colleges, even though she was smart enough to ace every class.

Grace was a free spirit. She lived each day with more enthusiasm than other's do with their entire lives. She wasn't directionless – in fact she was the most driven person I knew. But her desires did not match her mother's and that often caused tension between the two.

I could see that tension now in Grace's face. I wasn't sure if anyone else would pick up on it, but I knew every curve of her face, every expression. The minute jutting of her jaw and the squint of her eyes meant that she would rather be anywhere else but on display.

"Thank you all so very much for coming to help me celebrate my daughter's eighteenth birthday. I hope you are all having a wonderful evening." Sylvia turned and looked at her daughter, smiling gently. "I struggle to believe that it was eighteen years ago that Grace came into our lives. She's grown now. What a difficult predicament for a mother!"

Everybody chuckled politely.

"As mothers, we want to take care of our children, lead them along the right path. It is ingrained in our very nature. So, when that child becomes an adult, it's difficult to let go. However, it gives me great relief to know she is going straight into good hands."

I cocked my head to the side, confused. Had Grace finally told her parents about me? Was this their way of accepting me? A spark of hope lit inside my chest.

"I don't think she'll mind my saying, given we're among friends. So..."

I watched Grace's face fall.

What was going on?

The soft clack of footfalls caught my attention, and I watched Louis step up on stage and stand beside his daughter like a proud sculptor stands beside his greatest masterpiece.

"It is our great pleasure," Louis continued Sylvia's statement, "to announce to you all that Grace is set to marry our dear friend's son, William Carter."

The room erupted in applause.

I couldn't breathe. My skin burned, and my heart raced ferociously in my chest.

I watched a wealthy young man walk up on stage with a sheepish expression on his face. He bowed towards the crowd and laughed like he was embarrassed about the attention. He had deep brown eyes, almost black, and dark hair, with a brilliant smile and handsome features.

I felt entirely inadequate.

I looked nothing like this man. There was nothing spectacular about me. I had a mop of dark blonde hair, blue eyes, and a face that was ageing before its time.

I was not anything like... that.

William draped his arm over Grace's shoulder and her face was a mixture of ferocity and shock.

She met my eyes and I stared blankly back at her, before I remembered how to use my legs. I turned around, left the room and didn't look back.

Chapter Eight

I had been expecting the evening to be horrible, unbearable even. But in all the awful scenarios I had played out in my head, I had never suspected that I would walk away feeling like *this* after experiencing something as devastating as *that*.

Of course, I should have seen it coming. The angry voice in my mind chastised me for being so stupid, so vulnerable.

This is what happens when you let people in! You're not good enough for her! You got nothing more than you deserved. Fool.

I walked down the street that suddenly seemed miles long. My shadow revealed how low my head was hanging and my slumped shoulders, hunched in degradation and rejection. I traced my fingers through my floppy hair and brushed it back out of my face.

I realised that this was something I should have been prepared for. How else could this have ended? With a 'happily ever after'? I scoffed at the thought.

I didn't get 'happily ever after's. They weren't made for me.

With painful clarity, I saw the life that could have been mine flash before my eyes. It was the life that I thought would have been mine, just a few moments before my world fell apart.

I saw marriage, travelling the world, children, school functions and the dreary tasks of day-to-day life that I would have reveled in, so long as Grace was by my side. The slideshow ended with the two of us, old and decayed by the violent mistress of time, sitting hand in hand on the porch, overlooking the memories of a life well lived.

The weight of the agony felt enough to crush me, obliterate me. I wished it did.

I had never truly believed that love could be so deep, so quickly. When I looked around, love seemed sensible – more a matter of convenience, than desperation so unfathomable it was more important than your next breath.

Some would see it as a sign of immaturity, but I didn't blame them. It was only because they had never experienced what I had. What reason did they have to believe?

As I reached the car, I felt hollow. That was my chance at love and it was gone. I knew with a profound sense of certainty that I would not love again. It was Grace or no one at all. This realisation did not come from childish petulance or bitterness. I had experienced deep love and that is more than some ever received. I was grateful for my time and aware that it was now over. For how could I give another second-hand, second-best love? Wouldn't they deserve more than that?

"Jack!" I heard my name called, but I didn't want to respond. "Jack!"

I opened the door to my truck and got inside. I had turned the key to start the engine by the time Grace appeared at my door.

"Jack," she said breathless. "I'm so sorry. I don't know why she said that and I -"

"Okay," I said, cutting her off. I kept my voice steady, but it was flat and lifeless. "Congratulations and enjoy the rest of your birthday."

I pulled out onto the road before she had a chance to speak again. Her words of commiseration would sting more than the pain already churning my stomach, threatening to destroy me.

I threw myself into work like I never had before. I had cleaned up the mess in the garage in no time at all and was making swift progress at rebuilding the wall that had been destroyed by the fire. I expected to be finished in just a few days.

I worked from the moment I woke until the moment I crashed into my bed at night. I didn't want spare time to think, to mull over the gaping, bleeding wound that I feared wouldn't ever heal.

Three days after Grace's birthday, I received a letter from Frankie. I tore open the envelope and devoured the words.

Jack,
It's really not so bad here. So, I don't want you to be worrying about me. I'm staying with an older couple and Garret told me they're willing to have me stay as long as it takes. I suppose that's good. I don't want to be shipped around.
Lou-Ellen, the woman, is kind to me. Harry, her husband, teaches me how to mend things and chop firewood. They really treat me like I matter. And you were right – they do have a dog.
All the same, I'd rather be home with you. I wondered if you could tell me whether I'm right about something, Jack. Tell me the truth, without thinking of my feelings. Am I ever coming home? Or should I be prepared to stay?
Do you have plans to visit me soon?
Frankie
P.S. Mama says hello.

I hadn't yet found the strength to write back and tell him that he would be living with Lou-Ellen and Harry until he was an adult. I couldn't break him yet. Not with how broken I was.

I fumbled through rough drafts of my response in my mind as I hammered a nail into a board. Somehow, *Hey Frankie, our father is a selfish pig who won't give up the booze, so yeah, sorry, you're staying*, just didn't sound quite right.

I yelped as I brought down the hammer on my thumbnail. I shook out my hand as if this would somehow help and grumbled incoherent expletives.

I hadn't done anything more with the charred section of the garage but staple a tarp into place, until April tenth. I knew I would have to do it alone, as Robert was never in a state that I would trust him with a saw or hammer, and I would also have to shut the shop until I was finished. There had been too many bills that needed to be paid. But when I suddenly found myself with far too much free time on my hands, I closed the doors and set to work. The remaining bills would just have to wait.

I heard a faint tap on the door to the garage and leaned around a shelf to see who was there. My stomach dropped, and I immediately pulled back, hidden from sight.

Grace was peering in through the glass, searching for me. I couldn't speak to her. I couldn't face her.

I slid down the shelf and sat on the ground, waiting for her to leave. I shook my head in disgust. What a coward I was.

Finally, I heard the sound of her footsteps fading as she walked away.

Chapter Nine

Driving for six hours was exhausting. Especially when I was suddenly besieged by plenty of time to think. I tried to shut my mind up by thinking of how great it would be to see my brother. It didn't work.

As soon as Grace had left the garage, I ran to the house, shoveled some food into my mouth, packed my bags and left. I needed to get out, to get away from the constant reminders that I was alone, and that Grace was about to marry a man who wasn't me.

I knew that I was running away. But my sane mind had taken the backseat and was letting the broken man make all the decisions. I drove all through the night, resting only once on the side of the highway, and just for an hour.

The world coasted by me in a thick black fog, my headlights splitting the inky haze for just a few feet at a time.

Somewhere along the way, my agony turned into anger and my hopelessness turned into bitterness. How could she do this to me? What right did she have to break me like this? How could she string me along, letting me believe she loved me? Her actions didn't reflect the person that I thought I knew. I didn't understand.

I felt the fingers of my fury reach out to blame anyone else within my reach. I blamed Sylvia for revealing this hideous truth and for her influence over Grace. I blamed her father for floating along, a pacifist drowning in his own apathy. I added Robert and myself to the list of those at fault, slaughtering the hateful actions in the battlefield of my mind.

My hands choked the steering wheel as I fought to contain my rage.

Blinding tears stung my eyes and I wiped my face on my sleeves so that I could still see the road.

I let out a deafening roar that reverberated against the windows. All my frustration and pain bellowed out of me in a broken-hearted shout of defeat.

I had lost.

I slumped back against my seat and wondered if this pain could actually kill me, or just my mind.

The sunlight danced across my face, making me see bright red behind my closed eyelids. I blinked rapidly, waking from my deep slumber, and rubbed my eyes. I straightened and looked out the window of my car to the little house I had parked in front of when I arrived in the early hours of the morning.

The white house was surrounded by a small blue wooden fence, with a neatly maintained garden that was filled with roses. A cobblestone pathway cut through the grass, leading up to the front door.

I was glad that Frankie lived here. It seemed to be a better environment for him than any that I could offer. I looked down at myself and felt insecure, unwilling to get out of the car and knock on the door. I wore dirty, faded blue jeans and a grey button up shirt stained with sweat and sawdust. I hadn't changed clothes before I left home.

I reached around for my bag and pulled out a white shirt that was only slightly creased. I didn't look much better, but it was going to have to do.

To my surprise, I felt nervous. I didn't think that I had the energy to feel anything ever again. I opened the car door and stepped out. The weighty pain that I had experienced last night crushed my chest again, lingering in my bones.

I paused at the gate, giving myself enough time to ensure that I wasn't going to fall apart, before I unlatched it and walked in.

I knocked on the front door and scuffed my feet absentmindedly.

A pleasant looking lady, perhaps in her early fifties, answered the door with a curious look on her face. "Can I help you, young man?" she asked politely.

"Hello, ma'am, my name is Jack," I cleared my throat. "Uh, Jack Leatherby. I'm Frankie's brother."

"It's a pleasure to meet you, Jack." She smiled, and her face crinkled with delight.

"I know that it's rude of me to show up on your doorstep unannounced, but, I was wondering if I might be able to see him. Even if it's only for a little while."

The woman appraised me with a knowing look. I felt like a child in front of her. She nodded solemnly. "Of course, you can. He's outside with Harry. Why don't you come in and I'll get you something cool to drink? It's hot already out there."

"Thank you," I said, removing my boots and stepping inside.

The house had a homey feel about it, and I was instantly comfortable, as if I had been here a thousand times before. There was something safe about the house, and the woman who lived in it.

I followed her into the kitchen and smiled weakly when she passed me a tall glass of lemonade.

"Now, why don't you tell me what has you so low, Jack?" Lou-Ellen said, leading me back into the lounge room.

"I'm sorry?" I asked. How bad did my face look if she could tell from three seconds of seeing me that I was a wounded soul? I tried to rearrange my facial features to resemble something more at ease. It didn't work.

"Something has upset you, dear. I could beat around the bush for a while, as you painfully indulge me with small talk, but something tells me that you're in a place where you need a listening ear. Luckily for you, I have two."

I was speechless.

"So?" She took a sip of her lemonade and nodded at me encouragingly. "Go on."

Before I knew what I was saying, I was spilling out my painful, pitiful story. "You know when you think that everything you could ever want is right in the palm of your hands, but before you get a chance to grab hold of it, it's gone?"

She nodded.

"Well, that's...my...that's the story of my life." I felt the mutinous tears sting my eyes again and I sniffed, unwilling to allow this stranger in on my weakest moment.

"Love is not affectionate feeling, but a steady wish for the loved person's ultimate good as far as it can be obtained."

I rearranged myself on the seat. That was a painful thing to hear.

"C.S Lewis said that. It's very wise. But very brutal."

I chuckled half-heartedly. "It is. How did you know it was...love?" I sounded pathetic.

"Oh." She waved her hand and scoffed. "Everything is about love."

We sat in silence for a few comfortable moments. What was it about this woman that made me feel at peace?

"Sometimes when pain ripples through our chest, we feel like we'll never be the same again. A hollow void is left in the pit of our stomach and our minds bend our bodies to its will. Our chests ache, our limbs are stiff, and our appetite for life is destroyed. But it is when our broken pieces reflect the hope of a new day that the beauty in our pain is revealed."

"I don't feel like I'll ever be able to do that. It's just that...how can it be that love has such a power over us? It buckles my knees, fills my mind, and clouds my eyes. I don't know what to do anymore. How can I go home? Love is painful. I'm not sure I like it." I knew I sounded stupid, but Lou-Ellen nodded and smiled gently.

"Love is the strongest weapon mankind has at their disposal. It has the power to obliterate and reduce to ash, though it was never intended to do so. It was intended for something more potent than weaponry. It was intended for restoration. It is only since we got our sticky fingers on it that we used it to do damage. When it hurts, it's agonizing. But when it's right, there's nothing like it. When you get home, you must talk to her. Communication is the key. She might surprise you."

"I doubt it. She's..." I couldn't say it. I couldn't say that she was getting married out loud.

"Have you given her a chance to explain?"

"No," I said. "But, there's not much to -"

"That's not for you to decide, Jack. Give her the benefit of the doubt. If it is as you presume, at least you'll know for sure and when you're older, you won't look back and wonder. You can move on, knowing you've exhausted every avenue. How important can a love really be if it's not worth fighting for, worth making a fool of yourself over?"

My eyebrows crinkled together as I realised she was right. I hadn't given her the chance to explain, or apologise, or defend herself. How cruel I had been. I used to say that I would lose a thousand arguments if I had to. I would always go after her.

What happened to that man?

"Now, would you like to see your brother?" she asked happily, as if we had not had the intense conversation that had just passed.

"Uh, yes." I had almost forgotten I was originally here for Frankie. The conversation alone, with this intuitive stranger, was worth the six-hour trip. "Please."

Chapter Ten

I leant against the wall of the house, watching Frankie build a boat with Harry. He was still blissfully unaware that I was here, and I was pleased to see that he looked happy. He was laughing and smiling. I hadn't seen him laugh, really laugh, in far too long.

My mind was still reeling from Lou-Ellen's words. They were difficult to digest, but I knew she was right. I had to speak to Grace, let her explain. Then, when she told me she was to be with another, that her love for me had ended, I would, as C.S Lewis had said, wish for her happiness.

No matter how broken I would be without her.

Harry tapped Frankie on the shoulder and pointed to me, without saying a word. Their large dog started to bark happily. Frankie turned around, confused, and then he saw me. His jaw dropped before an enormous smile spread across his face. He threw the sandpaper he held to the ground and sprinted towards me.

I opened up my arms and he barreled straight into my chest, almost knocking me over.

"You came! You came!" he shouted.

I caught myself by surprise. I was laughing. I was happy. I felt a twinge of hope. Maybe I wouldn't love again, but maybe I could still find a way to be at peace.

I looked up at the kitchen window and saw Lou-Ellen smiling gently, as if she had known it all along.

"And then we went down to the park and they let me kick the football around until it was almost dark! When we got home, Lou-Ellen made meatloaf and potatoes and she let me have two helpings." Frankie was breathless when he finally finished bringing me up to date on everything that had happened to him since he arrived here.

I was so relieved that he was being well looked after. I was ecstatic that he was settled and enjoying himself. I couldn't have asked for more.

I fought to be alive for him for the two days that I stayed. I let myself laugh, joke, and smile. Hopefully he wouldn't notice my heavy heart if I disguised it well enough.

I had thought that it would be Frankie who would struggle with being away from home, who would struggle to leave behind his family. In truth, I had had much more trouble adjusting than he had. I appreciated his youth, his lust for life and his ability to adapt.

Lou-Ellen and Harry were remarkable people. They welcomed me into their family as if I was their own son. It was a strange feeling, to feel loved by a parental figure. It was something I could quickly get used to.

I found myself fervently wishing that Frankie really would stay here until he was an adult. Even if Robert sorted out his mess, he could not be to Frankie what Lou-Ellen and Harry were. Frankie had a chance at a great life, and I wanted that for him. Desperately.

I would break my promise. I would give up the fight. He needed to stay.

When it finally came time for me to leave, I felt lighter, more at ease. I knew Frankie was safe and loved and I had a plan for how to deal with life when I arrived back to reality in approximately six hours.

I pulled Lou-Ellen aside after shaking Harry's hand.

"I just want you to know that I really appreciate you taking care of Frankie. Both of you. It puts my mind at ease, knowing someone like you is looking out for him. I...I really hope he gets to stay with you. It's better this way." She could hear the pain in my voice and she put her hand on my arm reassuringly.

"He's still your brother, Jack. And you are welcome to visit him, and us, anytime you like." She lifted my chin with her forefinger and stared into my eyes. "I mean that. Anytime."

I nodded meekly. "Thanks. And thanks for your...advice. I really needed to hear it."

She smiled, and I hugged her tightly. It was strange. She reminded me so much of my mother.

"Okay, Frankie," I said, taking his shoulders in my hands. "I'll be back to visit you soon."

"Can I walk you out to the truck?" he asked.

"Sure."

We walked down the path, leaving Lou-Ellen and Harry in the house.

"Jack," he said when we reached the driver's side door. "About what I said in the letter - do you have an answer?" He was looking at the ground, avoiding my eyes.

"I do," I said softly. "You have a really great thing going here. Lou-Ellen and Harry are so good to you. They can offer you much more than we can. I think you'll be staying."

He nodded and slowly lifted his head. "Okay," he said bravely. "Okay."

"I'm gonna miss you, buddy." I hugged him tightly and ruffled his hair, fighting against the lump in my throat. I got into the car and wound down the window. "I'll see you."

Alone in the cabin of my car, no one could see my weakness. I didn't have to pretend or fight the emotions that ravaged me. As I drove off and looked in the rear vision mirror, I saw Frankie running down the street after me, holding onto me until he couldn't hold on any longer. The tears fell freely down my face.

Chapter Eleven

I had to go now, while Lou-Ellen's words were still fresh in my mind. If I didn't do it now, I would lose my nerve.

I pulled up in front of Grace's house and got out of my truck, not stopping to think anything through. I marched up to her door and my hand froze in a fist, just an inch away from the wood.

Knock, Jack. Knock!

I closed my eyes to gather myself and then knocked rapidly.

Sylvia opened the door and smiled grimly. "Can I help you?"

I could tell she remembered me from the party.

"Mrs. Lane, I'm here to see Grace. Would you please let her know that I'm here?"

She regarded me with something akin to distrust. "I'm sorry, but it is eight o'clock at night and Grace isn't receiving guests at this hour."

My stomach twisted. "I only need to speak to her for a moment. Please, Mrs. Lane. Then I'll leave, and I won't bother you again."

She pursed her lips before holding up one finger to me and walking away. The offer to disappear must have been too good for her to resist.

A few minutes later, I heard quick footsteps descending stairs. My heart quickened. How was I going to walk away after seeing her again?

She appeared in the doorway, taking my breath away. I almost groaned. It was too painful to see her; my heart was splintering in my chest.

"Jack," she breathed, pain and relief etched into her face.

"Hello, Grace. I realised that I should have answered the door when you came to the garage the other day. I'm sorry, that was cruel of me." My voice was formal, detached.

"No, that's okay. I..." she paused and looked to her left, where I was sure her mother was standing behind the door, listening to our conversation. "Let's go for a quick walk." She was out the door, closing it behind her before her mother would have had a chance to object.

She tugged at my arm and pulled me down the pathway onto the street.

"I didn't get a chance to explain," she said, letting go of me.

"It's fine. I understand. I don't fit into your world and William does. So, I just want you to know that I want you to be happy, Grace. I really do. So, if William is going to be the man to make you happy every day of your life, then I won't stand in the way." I wasn't sure if I sounded convincing. My voice was on the verge of breaking.

"No, Jack, you're getting it all -"

"Please, Grace. Don't. Just promise me that you'll take care of yourself and make sure that this guy treats you well, everyday -"

"Would you just shut up for a second!" she all but shouted at me.

I snapped my mouth closed.

"I understand why you left, why you didn't want to speak to me. But I've been going crazy! You left without giving me a chance to explain."

"What is there to explain, Grace?" I retorted. "You're getting married and you just forgot to tell me! I never thought you would do that to me!" I was supposed to be letting her explain and wishing her well for the future, but I was getting lost in my head.

I watched her expressions morph as I continued my barrage.

"What was I to you? Just someone to keep you occupied before you walked down the aisle? I love you, Grace, more than I ever thought possible. How could you do this to me?"

Tears fell soundlessly down her face, but I was too angry to stop shouting. "And at your birthday party! In front of everyone? Was that just so that you didn't have to tell me in person? Tell me, Grace, was it better this way? Did that ease your conscience?"

"No!" she shouted, rebuking my comment.

"Do you know what I have been through since you did this to me? Do you even care?"

"Yes! Jack, please. Stop!" She started sobbing.

"I thought I could do this," I said, holding up my hands in defeat. "I thought I could come here and wish you all the best, but I can't. I have to get out of here."

I turned and walked away, too angry to drive. My fists clenched by my sides. My heart was racing, and my head was pounding.

"Jack!" she called after me. "Wait!"

I didn't stop.

I heard her footsteps as she ran behind me, trying to catch up with my long strides.

"I'm not getting married, you idiot!" she called angrily. "Oh fine! Walk away, with your pride intact and just leave, why don't you!"

I stopped. Had I heard that right?

I turned around and faced her. She was ten feet away from me, huffing angrily with her arms rigid beside her.

"What?" I snapped. Acid was in my tone, my pain welling up and spouting out of my mouth.

"I said just walk away! Now! Get out of here!"

"No!" I yelled. "The other thing!"

"I said that I'm not getting married!" She looked away from me and shook her head.

"Not?" I barely whispered.

"No!" she was still yelling. "My mother had arranged it, and I told her, over and over again, that there was no way that I was going to marry someone I didn't love! She wouldn't listen. I never told you about it, because it was never a possibility, it was never going to happen. And believe me, the last thing I expected was for her to announce it at my party! The stupid party I didn't even want to have! I'm sorry that I never told you but -"

I cut her off, crushing my lips against hers after closing the gap between us in less than two seconds. I wrapped one arm around her waist and the other around her neck, pulling her closer to me.

Every agonizing morsel of pain that had filled my heart and mind dissipated, blowing away in the wind, as I became lost in her embrace. My heart was still racing, but with joy rather than fury and the pounding in my head vanished.

When I pulled away, gasping for air, I squeezed her tight and she wrapped her arms around my neck, sobbing.

"I'm sorry, I'm so sorry," she whispered.

I pulled her head back and kissed her again,.

Passionately. Enthusiastically.

"Marry me, Gracie," I said as I pulled away again.

"What?" she said, struggling to regain her breath.

"I'm in love with you. All I know is that I want to spend the rest of my life with you. I want to make you happy, every day. I want to see you smile when you wake up in the morning and I want to be the one that you share your dreams with." I paused and took a deep breath. "Will you marry me?"

"Are you sure? You're not just asking me because you thought someone else had?" Her voice quivered with the fear that my answer might be yes.

I smiled and pulled back from her. I bent down on one knee and looked up. "I'm asking you to be my wife, Grace Lane, because I love you. I will never love another person on this planet more than I love you. And I know it's crazy, because we haven't known each other long, but if you say yes, I promise I'll spend the rest of my life making you happy and making all of your dreams come true. I'll build you a house, if that's what you want. I'll take you around the world. I'll do whatever you want."

Her breathing became ragged as I took both of her hands in mine. I didn't feel afraid. This was what I wanted, and I would follow what Lou-Ellen said - if your love is real, then making a fool of yourself shouldn't matter.

Grace looked deeply into my eyes and I watched as her lips spread into a smile. "Absolutely."

Chapter Twelve

The sky was unnaturally blue. On a day as sad as this, shouldn't dark grey clouds cover the sky, with the threat of torrential rain and thunderstorms? Shouldn't I be standing in front of the lowering coffin with violent wind blowing my hair into my eyes and cold rain dripping down my face?

I should not be standing underneath a gloriously blue, cloudless sky, with the warm sun spreading its unwanted joy. The scene wasn't right.

The funeral was small. There were no more than ten people there, watching the coffin disappear into the belly of the earth. I thought there should be more people here for her, but apparently my great aunt was not as loved by everyone as much as she was loved by me.

She lived in London, but her body was shipped back to us, her only remaining family, to bury. She had offered to take Frankie and me to London with her when my mother passed, but Robert wouldn't hear of it. Back then he was too prideful to surrender us, to admit he couldn't do it without her.

I hadn't seen her for four years, but we wrote each other often. She was full of life and enthusiasm and her body never betrayed her by revealing her age. She had lived a long and full life and that's all anyone could ask.

I threw a single white rose – her favourite – into her grave as the men began to shovel in the dirt. I turned on my heels and walked away.

Frankie hadn't wanted to come. He had said that he wanted to remember her as she was, but I knew the real reason. The last funeral he went to was his mother's. He had no intentions of ever going to one again.

I sat underneath a tall tree with wide, reaching branches, in search of relief from the sun's hot rays.

I took off my suit jacket, rolled up the sleeves of my white shirt and loosened my tie. Evelyn wouldn't have cared if I wore jeans to her funeral. She was always running against the grain. I used to think that she loved to do things her own way just for the sake of it. She was young until the day she died of old age.

I chuckled to myself and shook my head.

"What's funny?" I heard Grace ask as she walked up to me, grinning at the expression on my face.

"Uh," I laughed again, more uproariously this time, causing horrified glares from the other funeral goers. "Evelyn would have hated this! She hated suits, ties and stuffy people. This would have been her idea of a nightmare!"

Grace sat down beside me and put her hand on my back. Soon my laughter faltered and gave way to the tears I had hoped not to shed.

I leant my head into her shoulder and attempted to stop the sobs rising in my throat.

"I know, Jack, I know," Grace whispered, holding my head in her hands. "I'm so sorry."

"Jack!" I heard someone shout my name.

I turned around and looked for whoever had called me. A short, plump man, wearing a grey suit was standing beside Robert, who had a furious scowl on his face.

"Oh, no. I'm in trouble," I sighed to Grace as I stood up, wiping away the tears on my sleeve. I kissed her cheek. "I'll be back."

I trudged across the grounds and stopped in front of the two men.

"Do you want to contain yourself?" Robert hissed at me. "This is a funeral.

You were laughing like this is all a big joke."

"Well, it kind of is," I said, trying to control myself. Trust Robert to miss the tear stains on my cheeks. "Evelyn would have hated this. She was never one to do things the way that everybody else did."

He scoffed and shook his head angrily, staring at the ground. "This is Mr. Thomson. He was Evelyn's lawyer. He wants to talk to us about the will."

"Tomorrow at ten would be best for me," Mr. Thomson said in his English accent, tapping his fingers against his leg nervously.

"Okay," I said.

"Excellent. Well, I will see you at your house at ten o'clock tomorrow. Good day." Mr. Thomson tipped his hat and walked away.

Robert looked up and glared at me. His eyes were glassy from the drink swimming in his veins and sweat dripped from his brow.

"I forgot to tell you," I said, tucking my hands into my pockets. "I'm engaged."

I watched his mouth pop open as I turned around and walked away.

I could have told him differently. Of this, I was certain. It was probably not an appropriate time and I could have prepared him a little - perhaps told him that I was seeing someone. He had no clue that Grace was in my life. Evidently, hearing that I was getting married came as a shock.

I wasn't sure why I hadn't told him earlier. I was at war with myself. I didn't want to care for him anymore. I wanted to hate him, to leave him to wallow in the mess he had made for himself. He had never done anything to deserve my love, so why should I freely give it, only to be wounded yet again?

I realised, however, that I didn't hate him. I couldn't hate him. He was my father, my flesh. I cared that he drank, that's why it made me so furious. I was gut-wrenchingly disappointed that he fed Frankie to the wolves and gave him up. And it was true that he had never done anything to deserve my love, to give me a reason to care for him. But that was not the point. It was up to me to make the decision about the person that I wanted to be.

If I let bitterness take me over, then I was no better than he was – allowing pain to dictate your future, to hold onto it with both hands because you couldn't imagine living your life without it, is not the way to truly live.

I had to let go. I had to let him go. I couldn't fix him, couldn't control him. I could only control myself and I was going to be a better person from that moment on. I was going to forgive him. Or at least try.

Even though the thought of it caused me physical pain.

I sat silently at the dining table, across from Robert, waiting for Mr. Thomson to arrive. I couldn't imagine what there was to talk about. Evelyn had lived a scrupulous life. She had never had a lot of money or possessions, and I was not entirely comfortable with the idea of dishing out a dead woman's belongings. It felt wrong.

There was a quiet knock at the door. I shoved back my chair and walked over to let him in.

"Thank you, Jack," he said, taking off his hat and stepping into the kitchen. "Thank you for making the time to see me."

He was such a nervous looking man. I wondered if he was like this all the time, or if something about us put him into a state of worry.

I smiled, hoping this might ease the tension. "Have a seat."

We sat around the table, unspeaking for a few awkward moments, until I poured myself a glass of water and offered him something to eat or drink.

"Oh, no thank you, Jack. We should get straight to business. As you know, Evelyn moved to England and I have been her lawyer for many years. She made up a will, which I brought along with me."

He dug into his black briefcase and pulled out a document. "Now, Evelyn had explicit wishes for her belongings after she passed. To you, Mr. Leatherby, she left the belongings of her niece, that is, your late wife. There are various artworks she made for Evelyn and a few other pieces that may be of interest to you."

I watched his face light up at the mention of unseen belongings of my mother's. He clasped the table to steady himself, as if the items were undiscovered pieces of her, which kept her heart beating inside his own chest, where it would be safe from the world, for just a while longer.

"To Franklin, she left her record collection, a valuable stamp collection, and monies totaling the amount of ten thousand pounds, to be kept in trust until he is of age."

My jaw dropped. Where did Evelyn get ten thousand pounds? My mind suddenly raced with the possibilities that would be opened for Frankie now, with money to help him later in life. I wished he was here. I would have loved to see his face when he heard the news.

"And Jack, I have a letter for you. She stated she would like you to read it immediately."

Mr. Thomson handed me a thick envelope with Jack written across the front in her flowing script.

I opened it carefully, as if it might disappear at any moment, and pulled out the letter.

My dearest Jack,

Well, I'm dead. Not to worry though, I'm in heaven, putting in a good word for you. I'm sorry that I never made it back to see you after your mother passed. I wanted to, but for some reason it never happened.

That's the funny thing about life, isn't it? You have to seize the moment, or the days keep passing and before you know it you've run out of time.

I'm sure my funeral was insufferable, but these things must be done I suppose. I don't want any mourning, or ridiculous tears. I'm old. It's alright. It was my time.

Now, on to more important things - you. Jack, my dear, you have to stop living your life for other people. The only one who has to deal with the decisions you make, is you.

Don't get to the end of your life and wish that you did everything differently. You get one shot here on God's earth and then you go home to heaven. So, make it count! I've watched, and read in your letters, how you put yourself last, every day of your life. It is a trait I admire in you, Jack, but it is a trait that worries me, as well. I want you to live – to actually live, every day like you mean it!

You can't do anything about the past, or the actions of others. But you have too much potential to squander your days picking up after people.

I love you, Jack. You're a good man. Don't you go forgetting that or neglecting yourself.

Enjoy my final gift. If you don't go just a little wild, I will be terribly disappointed.

Evelyn.

P.S. Give it away and I'll be furious... I mean it.

I folded the letter and chuckled to myself. It was so like her to begin a letter with '*Well, I'm dead.*' But I had no idea what her final gift would be. I took a sip of water as Mr. Thomson smiled.

"Excellent," he said. "Now, to you Jack, she left her house in London and monies totaling the amount of one million pounds."

I dropped my glass and it shattered into pieces.

What?

"I'm sorry, but, could you repeat that?" I said flatly.

"I said that Evelyn has left you her house in London and one million pounds." Mr. Thomson looked at me as if I was deaf or crazy or both.

"There's got to be a mistake," I said, shaking my head. "She didn't have that kind of money! I didn't even know she owned her own house!"

Mr. Thomson's brows creased together. "Yes, she has owned her own home for some years now. It's quite a lovely place, too. And as for the money, I believe she earned it all. She became quite a talented writer. When you travel to her...your...home, you'll see her books in the study. It's quite a large collection, actually."

My head was spinning. This was insane. I was...a millionaire?

"Well, here is my card. Mr. Leatherby, your items are still at Evelyn's home, and when I return to London, I will have them shipped over, along with Franklin's records and stamp collection. Jack, here is the key to the house and the deeds to the property. Your money will be wired into an account of your choosing. Call me and let me know the details. I have to leave to see Franklin now and let him know about his inheritance. If you have any questions, please, let me know."

Then Mr. Thomson was gone.

I was left feeling completely overwhelmed.

"So, Jack, are we going to talk about this?" Robert asked when I finally remembered how to stand up from the table.

"Talk about what?" I asked.

"About the money and what you're going to do with it."

"What do you mean?"

"Well, I think it's only fair that since Evelyn gave you the most amount of money, you help out your family. Frankie has ten grand for himself, so he's fine. But there's a mortgage on this place and the garage could -"

"You want me to give you the money?" I asked, cutting him off.

Robert stared at me. "That's not what I'm saying. But you live here too, and the garage is something you can invest in. It's part of your future."

I wrapped my fingers around the top of the chair. This was unbelievable and yet, expected.

"No, thank you." I kept my voice calm. "I don't intend to stay working at the garage for very much longer." I let out a deep breath and left before he could respond.

I was fuming when I made it to the Jeep, but I was adamant that I would put my frustration aside and be happy.

Maybe I could get out of this town now. I could actually travel and photograph all the incredible places I wanted to see. Grace and I could get married sooner than we planned, and we could spend our time travelling. The world was our oyster.

I broke more than one road rule as I rushed through town to get to Grace's house, making just one stop along the way. I beeped the horn when I arrived and jumped out of the truck. Running to her front door, I hammered my fist on the wood and tapped my feet as I waited impatiently for the door to be answered.

It was Sylvia. Of course.

"Hello Mrs. Lane. I'm here to see Grace." I was breathless.

She squinted at me and ground her teeth together. "Grace is busy."

"Mrs. Lane, I fully intend to marry your daughter. I love her, and she loves me and that's all that matters. I know you don't think well of me and there's not much that I can do that will change that. But you should be pleased in knowing that I love Grace more than I do myself. I will spend my life making sure hers is exactly the way she wants it. I have enough money to take care of us and she will be my bride. Now, if you'll kindly let my fiancé know that I am here, I would greatly appreciate it."

I heard a little *pop* as her mouth fell open. I didn't think she had ever been spoken to like that, but I had just about had enough of being treated like I didn't matter.

"Young man, I -"

"Mama, who is it?" I heard Grace ask.

I smiled pleasantly and called back. "It's me, Gracie."

She poked her head around the door and regarded me curiously. "Are you alright? You look all excited."

"I am," I said, grinning.

Grace squeezed out the door, ducking underneath her mother's restricting arm.

"Mama," Grace said, sounding sad. "We talked about this. This is what I want. I know you don't like it, but I do. Shouldn't that count for something? It would mean a lot to me if you could make an effort."

Sylvia fought to place a small smile on her face. "Yes, dear," she said curtly before she turned her attention to me. "Jack, won't you please come in."

"Thank you, Mrs. Lane, I'd love to."

We walked into the sitting room and Sylvia paused in front of the kitchen awkwardly. "Can I get either of you something to drink?" she finally asked.

"No thank you, Mrs. Lane," I answered.

"No, Mama, that's okay. I'll get us something later if we want it."

We stood there in silence for a few moments before Sylvia forced another smile to her face. "Well, I suppose I'll leave you two alone."

When she left the room, I turned to Grace and hugged her close to me.

"I can't believe it!" I said, kissing her cheeks over and over again until she laughed and squirmed away.

"What?" she asked, wiping her face with her sleeve.

"You told your mother!" I was even more excited about Sylvia's *almost* acceptance than I was about the money.

Grace nodded and smiled. "Of course, I did, Jack. We're getting...married. Can you believe it? Married! We're probably insane. We'll be living under a park bench or something." She paused and tilted her head to the side. "You know, even if we did sleep on a park bench, I don't think I would mind. People go their whole lives without finding what we have. What does geography matter?"

I wrapped my hand around her neck and pulled her face to mine until my lips found hers. My heart was racing, and my mind was working overtime. I knew that Grace didn't care for money or nice things but to hear her confirm it, just as I was about to tell her that we were millionaires, made me euphoric.

"Okay," I said, pushing her away. "Stop distracting me, I have to tell you something."

"Well, technically, you did the distracting. I'm innocent."

I laughed and sat down on the lounge.

"Jack, what is it?" Suddenly concern was lacing her tone and worry was in her eyes.

I took a deep breath. "Okay. Well, I had a meeting with Evelyn's lawyer today."

"I know, you told me."

"Yeah, and he was explaining her will; everything she left for us."

"Okay."

"Well, Robert got some of my mother's belongings that she had given to Evelyn, like paintings and such."

"Oh, that's beautiful. I bet he can't wait to sort through them."

"And Frankie got her music collection, stamp collection, and ten thousand pounds."

"Ten thousand pounds? That's amazing! Imagine how much it will help him! Jack, that's great!" Grace clasped her hand to her chest.

"I know. And she...well, for me...she left..."

"Jack? She left what?"

I sucked in three quick breaths, preparing myself. "She left me her house in London and ... One. Million. Pounds."

Grace was silent.

For a long time.

"Grace?" I asked, waving my hand in front of her face. "Gracie?"

"You...I....she left you...and that's...I..." she stuttered her way through a formless sentence and focused her eyes on mine. "Are you serious?"

I smiled and started to laugh. "Yes! I'm serious! Grace, she left us a house in London! And a million pounds! We can get married straight away! We can travel, just like you've always wanted to!"

"You can take photos!" she squealed, before wrapping her arms around me.

"There's just one more thing," I said, reaching into my coat pocket. "I didn't get to propose to you the way I would have liked to." I pulled out the object I had purchased on the way here.

I got off the couch and bent down on one knee. In my open palm was a small black box.

Grace sucked in a breath and tears welled in her eyes.

"Grace Lane," I said, opening the box to reveal a white gold band with a dainty diamond in the middle. "Will you marry me?"

"Jack! Yes! Of course, I will! What did you do? You shouldn't have spent this money!" She pressed her hands against my cheeks and kissed me.

"I had some money saved up. I was going to use it for the wedding, but I didn't need to anymore. I wanted to get you a ring. I wanted to do this properly."

I pulled the ring out of the box and slipped it onto her finger. Now all of the world could see that we belonged together, that I was hers and she was mine.

She held her hand up and inspected it, a look of incredulousness on her face. "Jack," she sighed. "I love you."

I grinned. "Gracie, you have no idea."

Chapter Thirteen

It was June 3rd and I was suddenly petrified. Not because today was my wedding day, but because I would be getting married in front of a lot of people. We had both wanted a small, intimate wedding, but Sylvia had insisted that she be the one to organise it.

"If I'm going to have to deal with this relationship, I had better be allowed to plan the wedding," she had said not long after I told Grace about the money.

We figured it was the least we could do since she wasn't kicking up as much a fuss as I had imagined that she would. She was acting as if she didn't entirely hate me.

Obviously, money does make a difference.

The plans for the wedding had been taken out of Grace's hands, but

she was still required to partake in a lot of the decision making. I barely got to see her for the two weeks before the wedding. That meant I had to keep myself occupied.

I worked more than was necessary, repairing cars until they were factory fresh - not just running – and restocking shelves that were already full. The small house I lived in had never been cleaner - and I had never been more restless in my life.

In my spare time, I worked on the final touches of our honeymoon. We would spend two weeks in Paris before we left for London and made a home for ourselves in our new, fully furnished house.

I couldn't have asked for a better start to our young lives together.

Grace's parents had insisted on paying for the wedding. I had objected, but Louis had put his foot down. "You're taking my daughter and fleeing to London. You can at least let me have this one thing. I'm paying for the wedding, like I have been planning to do since she was born, and that's the end of it!"

I hadn't brought it up again.

I straightened my bowtie. I was so uncomfortable, wearing this tuxedo. I didn't know how men did this all the time. I would have much preferred to be wearing my old jeans.

I heard a man clear his throat and I turned around to see Robert standing in the doorway. "You look good, son," he said. I could tell it was a difficult thing for him to say.

"Thanks," I said, adjusting my tie, yet again.

"Stop fidgeting. You'll do more damage than good."

I laughed half-heartedly. "Yeah, you're probably right."

He walked up to me and put his hand on my shoulder. I looked into his eyes and they were clear. His breath didn't smell of alcohol.

"Are you sober?" I asked without thinking.

His face pinched in pain before he controlled himself. "Yeah, sober. There are not many days that I want to remember anymore, but today, when my boy is getting married, is certainly one to recall."

I hugged him tightly, something I hadn't done in years. "Thank you."

He slapped my back and we parted. "You really love her?"

"More than is sensible, I'm sure of it." I looked down and kicked my feet along the carpet of the back room of the church.

"That's the best kind." He looked away and I knew he was remembering her, the love of his life. Then he said something to me that he used to say every day. "The Leatherby's only fall in love once, kiddo, so make it count."

I smiled and nodded, knowing how true it was. For generations, the men in the Leatherby family would marry once, and once only, even if their partner passed away. Something in our genes made us fall hard and fall once. I remembered the feeling when I thought I had lost my Gracie to another man. I knew I would never love again.

I was enormously grateful that it didn't matter anymore. She was mine.

"Are you ready?" Robert asked.

"I think so."

"Good, cause it's time."

The church was overflowing with people, most of whom I had never seen before in my life. I walked swiftly down the aisle and took my place in front of the minister. Frankie stood beside me, a giant smile on his face. When I had told him I was getting married, he had laughed and asked who my victim was.

Now he was beaming at me, glowing with pride as he stood as my best man. My eyes sought out the comforting faces of those I knew. I watched Robert take his seat in the front row and then saw Harry and Lou-Ellen. Lou-Ellen smiled at me knowingly and wiped her eyes with a handkerchief.

Sylvia, despite her prior objections, was smiling softly. Her makeup was already running from the tears that trickled down her cheeks. I smiled at her and felt my heart increase its speed when I heard the back doors creak open.

Grace's cousin, Mary, was her maid of honour. She wore a long, soft lavender dress, and her hair was wound gently atop her head. Everyone seated in the pews turned around and watched the procession.

She walked up slowly and stood opposite me with a lovely smile on her face, but I hardly noticed. My eyes were glued to the open back door and the empty space where Grace would soon appear.

She strode forward, into my line of sight, and my breath was stolen from my lungs. Her father held her arm in his and they stepped past the threshold, beginning their walk down the aisle.

The music began to play, but my heart was so loud in my ears that I could hardly hear it. I watched her walk gracefully towards me and I was suddenly overwhelmed.

Her hair fell loosely past her shoulders in gentle brown curls, with a wreath of small flowers braided around the top of her head. Her dress was pure white, reaching all the way to the floor, with a full falling skirt. Her shoulders were covered by the small white jacket that accompanied the strapless and intricately designed dress. She was astonishing to behold.

Her eyes locked on mine and I was held captive by her expression. She looked so peaceful, as if it were just her and me in the room. Her lips were spread into the softest smile and I couldn't believe she had chosen me. I couldn't believe that I would get to spend the rest of my life with her.

I wanted to run to her and sweep her off her feet, but I forced myself to stay still. She and her father stopped in front of me and Louis kissed his daughter's cheek.

The minister said something, and Louis responded, but I couldn't concentrate enough to understand them.

Grace stepped forward, as her father turned and joined his wife, and stood in front of me. She took my hands in hers and I was sure that this was a cruel dream. Any moment I was going to wake up and this would all just be a fairy tale. I didn't think that 'happily ever afters' could be mine.

The minister began to speak again, and this time I had to force myself to pay attention. I had to respond.

At some stage during the service, I repeated the words he spoke and said, "I do", but it was all a blur. Grace robbed me of the chance to remember it clearly by looking the way she did. I couldn't see past her intoxicating brown eyes.

"I do," she said, smiling.

I looked down and I was sliding her wedding band over her finger. Moments later, there was a ring on my hand, and I couldn't ever remember how it got there.

"You may now kiss the bride," I heard the minister say.

Finally.

I put my hand on her cheek and lifted her face to mine, kissing her gently.

The church erupted in applause and I realised it was probably time to pull away. Reluctantly, I released her and grinned widely.

We were married.

The reception was held in the town hall, which had been decorated beautifully, with white ribbons and gold trimming. The evening passed in a happy haze. I had never felt more alive. Yet, I still felt like I was dreaming. Could this really be happening? Could I really have the chance to be this happy?

I stood in the corner of the room, shadowed by the darkness, so I could have a moment to observe what was happening. I watched Grace circle the room, hugged by the women she passed and wished the very best by the men.

It felt so surreal. This event, these people – it was all here for us. I felt like I mattered, like I was somebody important.

"Are you having a good time?"

I turned around to see who had discovered my hiding place.

"I am," I replied to Robert as he stepped forward and allowed the shadows to engulf him. "I just...it doesn't feel real."

"Yeah, I know that feeling. Usually you're the one that's turning up to these kinds of things for others. Now it's all about you."

"It's weird." I surveyed the room and found Frankie dancing like a maniac with Sylvia. I stifled the hysterical laughter that threatened to break loose. Sylvia's face was twisted into a mixture of reluctant fun and horror.

"Son, you can stay watching the party pass you by, or you can walk in head first and be a part of it. That way, in many years from now when someone asks you about it, you'll know what to say because you were really and truly there."

I looked at his face through the darkness and smiled to myself. He was so different without toxic waste sliding through his veins. I almost...liked him.

"You're right," I sighed. "Let's party."

I stepped out from the shadows and into the light of the room. Grace spotted me immediately and called me over. I hurried to her side and took her hand, just as the lead singer of the band called out. "And now, for the first time, please make welcome Mr. and Mrs. Jack Leatherby!"

I took my wife's hand and led her onto the dance floor. The music flowed softly around us, and we twirled around. I was going to be present for this. I wanted to remember every moment of this day for as long as I lived, and then some.

"Are you happy?" I asked her.

"Very happy," she sighed contentedly.

"I love you," I said, kissing her forehead.

"You have no idea," she replied.

The dance floor filled with other couples as the music gave way to a faster beat. We didn't care. I held her close to me and we waltzed to the jive.

Through a shower of grains of rice, we headed down the stairs of the town hall. A sea of faces smiled broadly, and arms reached out to hug us goodbye.

I paused before my father's stiff frame and then wrapped my arms around him. Who knew when I would see him again.

Frankie was putting on a brave face, his lower lip trembling slightly. I might not see him for a long time either.

"You be good, okay?" I said, gripping his shoulders before pulling him close. "I think a trip to London is in your future, alright? I'll see you soon."

He smiled broadly, pleased at the offer of a free flight overseas. Perhaps he was just happy I wasn't going to forget him.

I took Grace's hand and we fell into the backseat of the car that would take us to the airport. We waved everyone goodbye as we drove into the black night, towards our very own happily ever after.

Chapter Fourteen

I smiled to myself as I remembered that night. My wispy white hair flopped around in the breeze and the sun continued to share its warm rays as we basked in the glory of a beautiful day. When you're old, you appreciate the little things more than you do when you're young. A day filled with good company and pleasant weather is the pinnacle of your existence. Every day has an opportunity to be the best day, because you are far more aware of the reality that life is short.

The vigor of youth has passed your body by and suddenly you realise that the years you've lived that seemed slow and sluggish at times, actually passed by in a whirlwind, a lightning-fast blur that left you with foggy memories as the only evidence that you once were different.

The saying that youth is wasted on the young is not so far from the truth.

I slowly lowered myself back until I was facing the sky, embraced by the grass. I didn't turn my head to see her, but I could feel Gracie smile at me. I hoped she was enjoying her birthday.

The blue sky loomed above me as fluffy white tufts rolled lazily along the earth's endless ceiling. I felt so small. So insignificant. What was I really? What was my time here on earth? A tiny blip in an everlasting age. Yet, everything felt orchestrated, designed. I was struck with the profound sense that my time mattered. Things would have been different if I was never here.

I didn't feel the need to speak. It was comfortable without words, almost as if we were having the greatest conversation without ever needing to utter a single syllable.

As in all marriages, we had difficult times. We were not immune to selfishness or stubbornness. I had a temper that I had to fight to control and Grace could act spoilt and entitled. We were both strong willed, with powerful personalities. Neither of us ever wanted to take the backseat or surrender in an argument. But these are things I rarely choose to recall, for the sweet times far outnumbered the bitter.

Every marriage has trouble, because it involves more than one person. There is bound to be friction when you have two human beings, whose very nature is self-centered, living side by side for all the days of their lives. It involves submission, humility, grace and forgiveness. These traits do not easily enter into relationships. It must be worked for, fought for.

The sign of a strong relationship is not found in the number of arguments. It is not measured by the good days versing the bad. It is the moment after, the next day. How you come out of the arguments. How you handle the pain filled days. A good relationship is defined by its ability to persevere.

At the end, you find something more precious than you could ever imagine.

I rolled over to face the picnic basket and pulled out a croissant. I had bought them from a bakery this morning, as a reminder of our honeymoon.

Two incredible weeks in Paris.

So far, I was thoroughly enjoying married life. We spent the first three days of our honeymoon staring out of our hotel window, wondering where to begin. I had ensured that we had a view of the Eiffel Tower from our room and we weren't disappointed. The city was beautiful. I had never seen anything like it.

Once we finally decided that we would have a better vantage point of the city's landmarks if we actually left the room, we explored every nook and cranny of the city, traipsing down each and every cobble-stoned street we could find.

The Eiffel Tower was amazing. I pulled out my camera and took shots from a hundred different angles. But nothing the city had to offer could compete with the look on Grace's face. She was absorbing every second, drinking in the moments. She was truly present, truly living. If I lived a thousand years, I would never be able to live a single day with as much passion as she did.

She turned to face me, her back to the tower, and smiled. She closed her eyes and took in deep breaths, clasping her hands to her chest. Pure bliss lined her smooth face. I snapped a photo of her without her noticing.

The steaming coffee sat in front of me, smelling gloriously tempting, but I couldn't look up yet. My pen scratched frantically at the paper of my journal, making my thoughts tangible and accessible to anyone I cared to reveal a piece of my mind.

I finished my sentence and threw down my pen, feeling triumphant. Grace returned to the table in time to see my success and laughed.

"Having fun?" She smiled and put her chocolate chip croissant down on the table before taking a seat.

"I've never really tried writing before, but I love it. Maybe I'll be an author or something." I picked up the coffee and took a sip to reward myself for my victory. It was well worth the wait. If Parisians knew anything, it was *le café*.

"You can use your pictures to go along with them," Grace said, suddenly sounding excited.

"Good idea." Though I doubted my pictures were good enough to be used, her faith in me was encouraging.

We sat in comfortable silence for a few moments before Grace reached out and took my hand. "Hey," she said softly.

"What is it? Are you okay?" I asked. I instantly felt sick in the stomach.

"No, I'm fine," she said. The knot in my stomach relaxed. "I was just thinking – this is it."

"What do you mean?" I asked, confused.

"This is it. This is life. We're in it. We can do whatever we want. We can make our life together look however we want it to. We can be anything. We're married. You and I are married." She said it as though it were a surprise, something brought upon her without her noticing.

I looked down at my left hand and gasped. "What the? How did that get there? I'm married? No!"

Grace giggled and reached across to punch my arm. "Stop it! You know what I mean. There's no one telling us what to do or who to be. We get to make our own decisions. Live our own lives."

I smiled at her and pondered her new revelation. She was right. For once, we were alone in the world and it wasn't a terrifying thought. We were allowed to just be. I squeezed her hand and leant across the table, pressing my lips against hers. When we parted, I sat back and grinned, thinking about the future.

Chapter Fifteen

Tomorrow we would be leaving Paris and heading to London. Our new house was waiting, but I was not looking forward to rummaging through Evelyn's belongings.

I had wanted to get everything I could from our time in Paris, and so far, had succeeded. We had spent the two weeks walking around in a blissful state, scarcely aware of the existence of others around us.

Other than Grace complaining of pain in the stomach, presumably from bad snails that we had forced ourselves to try the night before, our honeymoon had been without incident. It was as though the universe had paused, forbidding anything unpleasant to enter our atmosphere.

Of course, we had disagreed once or twice. My temper flared and Grace's spoilt attitude, that very rarely appeared, transformed her elegant self into someone I hardly recognised. But the spats were only ever momentary.

The sun had set behind the city and the sky burst into pale pinks and oranges, as a soft breeze danced around us. I took Grace's hand in mine as we strolled down the pathway and watched the world float by.

The streetlamps flickered on and illuminated us with a soft yellow halo. We had nowhere to go and nothing to do and it was brilliant. The night closed in around us and we walked, talked, kissed and laughed.

Paying no attention to the time, we walked on and once we realised it had long since grown dark, we sat on a bench overlooking an open park. I wrapped my arms around her to stave off the cold. She buried her head into my chest and I allowed my eyes to close.

I heard the trill of morning birds and snapped my eyes open. The world was the dusty grey of early dawn and eager joggers ran along the park's path in front of us. I looked down and saw Grace asleep, her head resting on my lap. I chuckled to myself – we had slept the night on a park bench - in France.

I didn't want to disturb her, so I sat still, watching the world wake up. I allowed my mind to wander and found myself thinking about my mother, and how much I wished she could have been there on my wedding day. Would she be proud of the man I had become? Or would I be a disappointment? Had I accomplished enough? Had I been a good guardian to Frankie?

I looked down at Grace and felt the crushing pain Robert must have felt when my mother died. If he loved her anywhere near as much as I loved Grace, then I could understand why he still dealt with so much raw and unmanageable pain.

I couldn't bear the thought of losing her. How could someone ever come back from that?

I shook my head in an attempt to dislodge the thoughts that had formed in my mind and gently pulled out my journal and a pen.

June 17th, 1958

The world is pale, the vibrant colours of a new day yet to rise from their slumber. Grace sleeps soundly beside me, her head in my lap. We slept the night on a park bench that overlooks small green hills that roll up and down like the ocean's waves. I feel like I am a part of this city. As though it is made up of living entities, not buildings and famous landmarks, and I am one insignificant part of its beating heart.

Joggers run past me, far too eager for their own good, their pounding feet keeping time with their heavy breaths.

I look up to see the first bold rays of sunshine that break over the horizon. The sky changes colour and its beauty is indescribable.

I paused from my writing and snapped my journal closed. Grace would want to see this. I shook her gently and cooed her name. She blinked softly and smiled. "Good morning," she sighed before her mouth popped open with the realisation she was staring at the sky and not a hotel room ceiling. She sat up quickly and looked around, sleepy shock on her face.

I laughed. "It's okay, Gracie. We just fell asleep here. But look -" I pointed out to the horizon. "I thought you might want to see the sunrise."

The shock on her face settled and she smiled, leaning back and resting her head against my chest. "You thought right."

The sky lit with the golden rays of first light as the sun slowly made its ascent. The noises around us increased as the world awoke, and more people began filling the streets. I wrapped my arm around her and rested my head on top of hers.

We were just two people in the eyes of the world. Our lives were inconsequential to the multitude that passed us by during the course of our park bench morning. Our past was a mystery to them, our futures unknown. We were just nameless faces. Just another lovesick couple in the most romantic city in the world.

It was strange to think that just this morning we were in Paris. Now we were standing outside of our new place in London. The house was enormous. And fully paid for. I could hardly believe that we could be this blessed so early in our married life. We pushed open the gate, ready to see our home for the very first time.

There was a neat garden lining a cobblestone path that wove its way straight up to the four steps that led to the porch. A stone chimney jutted out from the roof that stood two storeys above us. Large grey bricks formed the walls, making the house appear as though it were a large, rustic cottage. Lace curtains hung from the four or five visible windows and a porch swing sat just to the left of the door.

Hopping up the steps, I reached for the key in my bag to unlock the front door.

A mixture of excitement and dread coursed through me at the prospect of going inside. Would it be like walking into a tomb? Evelyn's belongings sat, untouched and neglected, waiting for the return of their owner. Everything would be sitting just as she had left it.

I made up my mind at that moment to make this house our home. Evelyn would not have wanted us to creep around the house she had left for me as if it were not our own, as if we were passing, unwanted guests.

With a deep breath, I opened the door and walked inside. Grace waited at the threshold as I walked into the foyer. I scanned the room with sad eyes and I could almost see Evelyn walking around, watering her plants and shuffling around the books in the massive bookshelf at the end of the room in front of me.

"Thanks Evelyn," I whispered.

I turned around and smiled at Grace, still perched under the doorframe.

"Gracie, this is our home. You can come inside."

"I just wanted to give you a minute."

I walked up to her and whisked her into my arms. "Would you like to see your new house, Mrs. Leatherby?"

She wrapped her arms around my neck as I supported her weight in my arms. "I would."

The foyer led on to a large open room that was filled with more than just the one bookcase. Hundreds of books filled the room and a huge fireplace took up an entire wall.

In the very centre of the room was her desk. Papers were strewn across the surface and an empty coffee cup sat on a thick pile. Directly across from her desk was a bookcase that stood out from the others. Its wood was darker, its build sleeker. I stopped in front of it and let out a deep breath.

At least fifty books lined up against each other had her name written on the covers. She really was an author. I remembered her telling me once when I was young that she wanted to write. I smiled, touching the spines of the books.

"You did it," I breathed.

From that room we walked through to the kitchen, full of pots and pans hanging from the centre of the ceiling, and gradually through the other rooms that made up the house.

As we ascended the stairs and traipsed along the hallway, I heard something thud behind me.

I turned and saw Grace crumpled on the floor, her hands wrapped around her stomach. Her face was pale and beads of sweat covered her forehead.

"Grace." I dropped down beside her and lifted her face to mine. "What's wrong?"

She grumbled something I couldn't understand and tried to get up. Her legs buckled underneath her, and I caught her before she crashed against the ground.

"It's okay," I said, worry gripping my stomach. "Come here."

I wrapped one arm under her knees and the other around her waist, lifting her up off the ground. She began to shiver in my arms as her head lolled back against my shoulder.

I walked as quickly as I could to the bedroom, trying not to jostle her in my arms. She squirmed uncomfortably, so I tried to put her down on the ground. She swung her legs and put her hand to her mouth. Her feet hit the floor and she stumbled. I picked her up again and took her to the adjoining bathroom.

She threw herself against the basin and heaved.

I sucked in deep and terrified breaths, pressing my palms against my forehead and raking my fingers through my hair. What was wrong with her?

I didn't think she would be pregnant and even if she was, morning sickness wouldn't come this soon. Anyway, this was nothing like morning sickness. She was ill. Desperately ill.

When she had finished, she tried to turn the tap. She was too weak. I reached over and turned it for her, as she rinsed out her mouth.

She wrapped her arms around me and coughed violently. With panic tearing at my heart, I helped her over to the bed and pulled back the covers. Lowering her in, I saw a trickle of blood running out of the corner of her mouth. A box of tissues sat on the bedside table, so I reached over, plucked one out, and wiped the red liquid away.

Her teeth chattered together, and her lips were turning blue. I had no idea what to do.

There are difficult moments you come across in life, which you can only hope you'll handle well. You hope you'll be calm, precise and wise. I was anything but.

I ran down the stairs like my shoes were on fire and frantically searched until I found the telephone. With my fingers hovering over the face, I paused...who should I call?

I didn't know this country. I had never been here before. What number should I dial?

I dropped the phone and ran to my bag by the door. Ruffling through it with shaking hands, I found the crumpled card.

I dashed back to the telephone and dialed the number.

Seven lethargic rings later, he answered.

"This is Mr. Thomson."

"Mr. Thomson! It's Jack Leatherby," I cried into the receiver, grateful for Evelyn's lawyer's response. Words spilled out of my mouth so quickly even I couldn't understand what I was saying.

"Jack, slow down, slow down. I can't understand you," he replied.

I took a deep breath and steadied myself before I spoke again, this time much slower. "I need your help. We're here in London, but Grace, my wife, is sick. I don't know what to do. I didn't know who else to call. We don't know anyone. Please."

"I'll be right there."

Then the line went dead.

Twenty minutes later, while I was kneeling on the floor beside the bed, holding Grace's hand and watching her rapidly deteriorate, I heard a quick knock at the door.

I stood up, kissed her forehead, and sprinted down the stairs, nearly tripping on my feet on the way down.

The door opened to reveal Mr. Thomson, accompanied by a man with a black briefcase and a bowler hat.

"Come in," I ushered them, stepping aside.

"Jack, this is Doctor Shore, a good friend of mine. He's going to take a look at Grace, alright?"

I nodded and pointed upstairs, unable to speak. Doctor Shore smiled politely and hurried up the stairs.

I fell back on the two-seater lounge that sat just inside the doorway and dropped my head into my hands.

Mr. Thomson sat beside me, rigidly. "It will all be alright. You'll see." Tiny traces of concern were in his voice, as if he didn't quite know whether to believe his own words.

"I...I can't lose her. Not now. Not yet. We...we've only just gotten married. I..." My words trailed off until they were quieter than a breath.

"Come now, she'll be alright. You mustn't think like that. For all we know it could be a common cold."

"There was blood...coming from her mouth." I could hardly form the words. With the little knowledge I had of human anatomy, even I knew that was a terrible sign.

Mr. Thomson didn't have a response. He just stiffly patted my back, his resolve crumbling ever so slightly.

"Thank you for coming," I whispered.

"Not at all, my dear boy. Not at all."

The time it took for the doctor to return down the stairs, was the longest I had ever endured. My mind had had enough time to conjure the worst possible outcomes, and taunt me with their viciousness.

I heard his light footsteps descending the stairs, and I looked up to see a worried expression on his face.

I stood to my feet and went to his side. "What's wrong with her?" I asked desperately.

"I can't say," he replied. "But I can tell you, that in her condition, it all depends on the next twenty-four hours. I've given her everything that I can. There are pills beside the bed with instructions for you."

"How can you not know? What about the hospital?" I asked.

"I don't think moving her is the best idea. Besides, she'll be more comfortable here." He put his hand on my shoulders and smiled sympathetically, as if he hadn't noticed my acid tone.

"So...?" I asked, drawing my own conclusions.

"Just be with her," the doctor said. "Don't lose hope. Nothing is written in stone."

I died just a little bit in that moment.

In a haze, I saw them out and stumbled back up the stairs. My Gracie was lying flat on her back under the bed covers.

Nothing is written in stone, I told myself over and over.

I couldn't believe that it was a possibility that she was going to die.

She smiled weakly upon my entrance and tried to move. At the tiniest movement, she began coughing violently. I hurried forwards and reached my hands out to support her.

"Stay still, Gracie," I whispered.

Another trickle of blood dripped down her chin. I reached for a tissue and wiped it away.

"I'm sorry," she rasped.

"What for?"

"Not telling you earlier."

My stomach dropped.

"What do you mean? Have you been feeling this ill for a long time?" My voice broke.

"For a while," she sighed sadly.

"Grace," I breathed. "I could have gotten you help sooner."

"I just wanted it to be perfect. I didn't want the wedding to be postponed.

But don't worry yourself." It took so long for her to say the words, as if simply speaking was expelling more energy than she had left.

She lifted her shaking arm, her hand heading towards me. Her face twisted with exertion, so I reached out and took her hand, carrying it to my lips. I kissed her palm before pressing it against my cheek.

"I'm going to be okay, Jack. You'll see."

"I know," I lied. "I know."

I didn't know. I didn't know *anything*.

The moon shone its silver glow into the room through the thin curtains, illuminating Grace's face in a ghostly pale silver. Her chest heaved up and down with every shallow and ragged breath that she drew in.

I didn't sleep a wink. I stared at her motionless frame, listening for each breath, watching for any twist of pain or heart beat's hesitation.

I had wrapped my world around her. She was too young, too full of life. She had too much yet to do, for her life to be lost now.

I wouldn't allow it. I knew that I had no control, but it made me feel a little better to pretend that I did. I held onto her with everything I had, held onto her life with a ferocious intensity. I couldn't let her heart stop beating.

Couldn't. Wouldn't.

Painful hours passed and suddenly her eyelids fluttered, and her deep eyes were boring into mine. I leaned forward and smiled.

"Hey Gracie," I sighed. "What is it?"

"Nothing," she answered after a while.

"Are you in pain?"

"Not so much anymore. I can handle it." Her voice was croaky and hoarse.

I couldn't believe how quickly this was happening. Where had this sickness come from? This wasn't right. This wasn't fair.

"Can I get anything for you?" I asked, traces of helplessness and despair lacing my voice.

Weakly she shook her head. "You-," she began before a vicious cough broke free of her chest. She gasped for breath, clutching at the bedspread as if it were a villain who refused to surrender the air supply she so desperately needed.

I leant forward and put my hand on her sweaty forehead.

"You took a chance on me, Jack," she breathed when the coughing subsided. "I never understood what you saw in me. But, I wanted to say-"

"Grace, don't," I said, cutting her off. "Don't. Don't do this. I can't. Please."

She held out one finger and pressed it against my lips to silence me. "I wanted to say thank you for loving me and showing me parts of the world I never would have seen without you. Wouldn't want to see without you."

"Grace, stop. You're gonna be fine, remember?"

Now it was her turn to lie. "I know, Jack. I know."

Moments of horrific silence passed between us. My heart drummed inside my chest, the sound pounding in my ears. My breath came in quick and ragged huffs and my shirt stuck to my back, wet with sweat.

"I've been thinking," I said, trying to distract myself.

"Mmmm," she moaned, too weak to respond with words.

"When you get better, we should go away again. Anywhere you want. Why stay here? We always wanted to go see new places and I thought that I could photograph them as well. Maybe write about our adventures overseas. What do you think?"

She smiled weakly and closed her eyes. "Havana," she whispered.

"What?" I leaned my head close to her mouth, so I could hear her.

"Havana," she repeated.

I chuckled. "Why Havana?"

"I've always wanted to go. It's supposed to be beautiful."

"Okay." I smiled weakly. "Havana it is. You rest, and I'll start planning."

I kissed her clammy forehead and sat back. I bit my bottom lip and resisted the urge to fall apart. "I love you, Gracie. More than you'll ever know. Sleep now."

She sighed softly and breathed the words "You have no idea."

I brushed her hair out of her face and sat back in the chair. I watched her sleep while I planned our Cuban escape, knowing we would probably never get the chance to live it.

Chapter Sixteen

We had been told by the various travel agents we had sought information from, that *La Habana* was a tropical paradise. Tourists were welcome, the people were happy, and the weather was perfect.

Upon arriving in Havana, I got the distinct impression that they were right about only two of those three. Underneath the façade of holiday bliss, there were aching people, who lacked basic rights and freedom. There was tension in the air, terror lining every Cuban face.

I had no idea why.

It was late December 1958 and Grace had been back on her feet for a few months now. When she claimed she was well again after a lengthy stay in bed, I suggested we stay in London for just a little longer under the pretense of English exploration. My real reason, which I feared was not lost on her, was that I was afraid she was going to crash again. If she was going to be ill, I wanted her to be somewhere comfortable – safe in her own home.

When I couldn't put it off any longer, we packed our bags and disappeared.

Havana was beautiful, but I couldn't ignore the feeling in the atmosphere, or the heavy police presence.

But as I watched foreigners walk down the street with happy smiles on their faces, carrying out their daily lives or soaking up the last days of their holiday, I saw that there was no unrest in their faces. I must have just been crazy.

Grace gripped my hand as we walked past the beach and looked up at me, smiling. I wanted her to truly experience life. That was all she had ever wanted – to live. As she had told me once in a courtyard, one night that felt like a lifetime ago, she wanted to touch, taste, see and hear everything the world had to offer.

It became my mission to help her succeed.

For the first week, we did nothing but eat and walk around. There was food everywhere you looked. On Christmas Day, we prepared an enormous picnic basket and sat down by the beach. With year-round tropical weather, we lounged on the sand and basked under the sun, with no concern of a wintery bite.

For the second week, we decided we had walked far enough down the tourist's road. There was more to this city than the foreigners wandering around in masses knew, and we wanted to discover what it was.

That was when we met Joaquin and Catalina. Joaquin was born and raised in Havana, six feet tall, tanned and addicted to his country. Catalina was a stunning Cuban dancer, set to marry Joaquin in the New Year.

As I had assumed, we hadn't yet experienced the true Havana. Not in the least.

"How do you expect to get a taste for *La Habana* when you're stuck in your hotel rooms?" Joaquin asked us, his thick accent highlighting his words.

"You need to come with us." Catalina nodded at us knowingly, as if she was privy to some great secret that had evaded us.

"Where to?" Grace asked, her eyes wide and excitement in her voice.

"*Danza y música*," Catalina cooed, savouring the words on her lips as if they were a fine wine.

I didn't need a translator to know what that meant.

I hadn't spent a lot of time in clubs in my time, but Cuban clubs were like nothing I had ever seen, and the music was indescribable. The passion in the air was unmistakable.

Catalina and Joaquin swooped onto the dance floor like they owned the place and blew us away.

When Grace and I tried, Catalina smiled like we were little children playing, and Joaquin just laughed.

"*Esta no es bueno, señorita,*" Joaquin said, still chuckling. "You have to get closer. You're married, *si*?"

"Yes," Grace said, blushing.

"So, then where is the problem?"

"It's so...different," I said, watching everyone around us.

"Different good or different bad?" Catalina asked.

"Good," I said, sounding unconvincing.

Truthfully, it was amazing. I wanted to be able to dance like Catalina and Joaquin could, but I would need some serious practice.

We stayed at the club for hours. Joaquin introduced us to his friends and Catalina showed us dozens of dance moves we were sure to never remember. The Cuban people were passionate and lively. I wanted to know where their zest came from, their ability to unwind.

They seemed to have perfected the art of simple pleasure.

It was around three in the morning when we left the club on the first evening we spent with our new Cuban friends. We walked down the street in the sticky night air, as Joaquin sung Spanish love songs and twirled Catalina around.

Hoping I wasn't going to offend, I asked the question that had been on my mind since we arrived in Cuba.

"Why does everyone here seem so afraid? Why is there such a heavy police presence? Everyone in the club seemed so free, but out here..." I trailed off.

"You don't know?" Catalina asked, surprised, stopping mid-twirl.

"No," I answered, shaking my head.

Catalina and Joaquin exchanged curious glances, before Joaquin spoke. "*Presidente* Batista. He makes it very good for everyone but the Cuban people. It is especially bad for the young people of Cuba. *Universidad de La Habana* shut down on November thirty, 1956, after a riot. People died. It was horrible. I used to go to university, but they shut it down to stop any, how do you say? Uh...'Revolutionary thinking'. It has not been open since."

"Why is no one doing anything about this?" Grace asked.

"Fidel Castro is trying to. There's talk of a, what do you call it? A coup? But no one really knows if they'll succeed until it happens, right? Until then, every young person is seen as a threat, someone who might be a revolutionary. Someone who believes in free Cuba! The government is so corrupt. They use violence to make people afraid of them. Cuba is run by mobs and gambling is their fuel."

I was speechless.

Every night that followed, we met up with Catalina and Joaquin. They led us around town and we began to feel like real Cubans. Every now and then, we received sidelong glances from Cubans who didn't know we thought differently than the other tourists that populated their country, but Joaquin would tell us it was all alright. They would take care of us.

Havana was alive. When the people were free to live, to be themselves, to be Cuban, there was nothing like it.

On the night of New Year's Eve, we had planned to meet a few of Joaquin and Catalina's friends. They were going to show us just what it was like to really celebrate like Cubans. I thought that was what we had been doing, but apparently, that was just a warm-up.

At sunset, Grace and I met the couple on the beach. Catalina took Grace by the arm and led her ahead of us, chatting on about this and that. Joaquin and I lingered back, strolling along behind our effervescent companions.

"It is the New Year, Jack. You are not celebrating with your family?" Joaquin asked.

"No," I answered. "It's just Grace and me. Our families are back home. My father's probably passed out on the lounge by now. I doubt he remembers I've gone."

"You don't have a good relationship with your father?" Joaquin questioned.

"Uh, no, not really," I mumbled.

"Oh. That is a shame," Joaquin responded, staring at his bare feet as they squelched in the moist sand.

"What about you and your father?"

"Well, I did. He," he paused and shrugged his shoulders. "He died when I was fifteen."

"I'm sorry. My mother died as well."

He looked up at me and pursed his lips in dissatisfaction. I could see sincerity swimming around in his eyes and we didn't speak until the sun had nearly fully disappeared behind the horizon.

"My father gave me something on the day that he died," Joaquin said, fishing around in his pocket. "I carry it with me all the time."

"What is it?" I asked as he pulled a folded piece of paper from his pocket.

"A list," Joaquin answered smiling.

As he unfolded the worn paper, I saw a numbered list scratched into the surface.

"What for?"

"He always said to me that the greatest tragedy in life is not that men die. But there is sorrow in death when he first had not lived. So, my father made me promise him that I would live each and every day that I was given. He gave me a list of all these things he wanted me to do and experience before I die."

He skimmed over the list and folded it again, slipping it back into his pocket.

"What do you think?" he asked.

"I think it's great," I answered. "I agree with him. Life is meant to be lived, isn't it?"

Joaquin looked at me and smiled. "*Si. La vida es para vivirla.*"

Life is for living.

Chapter Seventeen

There was chaos in the streets.

I had never seen a city thrown into bedlam in such a short amount of time. The parking meters were clobbered with baseball bats by frenzied Cubans and Molotov Cocktails were thrown through the air, crash landing in a fiery blaze. The sudden change in the air poisoned the environment, making it thick with fear and excitement.

It was the early hours of January first, 1959, and *Presidente* Batista had stepped down and decided to flee the country.

When Joaquin and Catalina heard the news, we were still out, celebrating the beginning of a new and hope filled year. Our Cuban companions were ecstatic.

Grace and I were terrified.

It was no longer safe to be on the streets. The police were hiding inside their stations, letting the mayhem wash over the city streets, refusing to step in. Grace and I were in danger, especially considering we were not Cuban. We were tourists. *Gringo.*

"Joaquin, we have to get back to our hotel!" I called out through the havoc.

"We will take you back there!" Joaquin shouted at us over the noise. "It is not safe for you to be alone!"

We made our way through the hectic streets, avoiding the violence and pandemonium. People were destroying anything and everything in their paths.

"They are destroying houses of people who love Batista," Catalina informed us as we raced past a home that was being set alight.

I heard car windscreens shatter and blood-curdling screams and shouts. I watched people run down the streets with odd household possessions, such as lamps and air conditioners. I couldn't imagine why.

Grace and I ran close to Catalina while Joaquin ran behind us. They had sandwiched us in for better protection.

A familiar voice shouting out in pain and the distinctive crunch of a car accident froze my feet to the spot. I turned around, unable to breathe, and saw Joaquin pinned between a building wall and the crumpled bonnet of a car.

"Joaquin!" I shouted over the noise, catching Grace and Catalina's attention. I turned and ran back to him, trying in vain to yank the car away and free his trapped body.

The driver was unconscious at the wheel, a heavy river of blood oozing down his forehead.

"Jack," Joaquin mumbled, barely audible over the noise.

I stopped trying to tug at the car and went to his side. I felt my stomach heave at the sight of him. A thick pool of gooey blood lay around his feet and the car had rammed into him with such force that his torso seemed only inches thick.

Unnatural, bent.

One hand was pinned under the car, trapped in a mash of metal, so I took his free hand in mine and squeezed it tightly. We couldn't move the car. In a horrible twist, it was the only thing keeping him alive. Catalina shrieked in horror and ran to his side, screaming and sobbing.

"I guess I'm not going to get a chance to live after all," he gasped, his face draining of colour.

"Grace, try and wake up the driver!" I shouted at her over my shoulder. She was frozen in place, stunned. "Grace! The driver!"

She snapped out of her shock, nodded and ran to the driver, shaking him aggressively.

"Yes, you are Joaquin," I said, gritting my teeth. "Don't talk like that. We'll get you out of here. We'll call someone who knows what to do. You'll make it." The lie tasted bitter in my mouth.

I could hear Catalina wailing and screeching incompressible words in Spanish as she stroked his face. Tears cascaded down her cheeks as the euphoric crowds carried on, unaware of the enclosing tragedy.

Joaquin smiled at her gently, as if it was all going to be okay, before turning back to me. "In my pocket," he rasped. "The paper."

"What?" I reached into his coat pocket, feeling through sticky blood as I searched for the list. I pulled my hand free, holding the paper that had somehow managed to stay white. My hand, however, was red.

"You take it and you finish it for me," he said. I had to lean close to hear his shaking voice. "Please, Jack. Finish it for me."

I pulled back and fought against the lump in my throat and the tears in my eyes. "I will. I promise. I will."

Joaquin smiled peacefully and turned back to Catalina. "*Mi amor. Te adoro. Te amaré por siempre.*"

I placed Joaquin's hand in Catalina's and stepped back. I shouldn't be privy to their private pain.

"*Te amo, te amo, te amo,*" she whimpered back. Catalina held onto the last moments she had with her partner, her vision blurring with falling tears. "*Te amo,* Joaquin."

As the light faded from his eyes and his body became limp, I felt a crushing, sickening weight on my shoulders. He died keeping us safe. No one should have to make that sacrifice.

I looked down at the paper in my hands. Time froze for a moment and I lingered in the stale taste of death. It was as if the world had paused, surprised at the tragic loss of one so young, before it shrugged its shoulders, and carried on.

"Grace," I finally said, putting the list into my pocket. "Stop."

She was still shaking the driver. At my words, she looked up at me, her face wet with shed tears. She stepped back, surrendering. Her face crumpled in pain and she reached over to take Catalina's arm.

"We have to go," she whispered.

"No!" she called back, shaking Grace off.

"Catalina," Grace said more forcefully. "It's not safe. We have to go. Now."

Grace pried her away from the wreckage, but she just dropped to the ground, scraping her bare knees on the rough surface. She clasped her hands around her stomach and screamed, her voice breaking with emotion.

I leaned down and took her hand, pulling her to her feet.

"No!" she shouted. "I'm not leaving him!"

Waving her hands violently, shoving me away, she fought to stay by Joaquin's lifeless side. I couldn't leave her there. She had to move. It wasn't safe.

I bent down and scooped her up in my arms, maintaining my grip around her knees and waist as she struggled in my hold.

"No! Jack! No! Let me stay!"

As I began to walk forwards, she reached over my shoulders and extended her arms towards the fading sight of her fiancé, dead in the street.

"I can't," I whispered, my voice almost nothing in the violent air. "I'm sorry."

"Joaquin!" Catalina cried out, over and over.

I looked across to Grace, who walked quickly beside me, shedding heavy tears.

Catalina began to punch my chest, lost in the shock and dying in the pain.

I could only keep walking.

Eventually her fists stopped striking and she went weak in my arms.

"No, no, no," she kept mumbling, pushing her face against my throat and weeping unrelenting tears. "No. *Por favor. Esto no puede estar pasando.*"

There was nothing I could do, nothing I could say, that would change the horror we had just witnessed. I held Catalina in my arms, kept Grace by my side, and navigated our way through the minefield that had become Havana.

Chapter Eighteen

I twisted and turned the paper around in my hands. I had not uttered a word for the entirety of the flight. The events of the first day of 1959 loitered like a sour taste in my mouth. I leaned forward in the seat and pressed my head into my hands, desperately trying to rid myself of the image of Joaquin's lifeless, motionless body that had been seared into my brain.

Every time I closed my eyes, I saw the blood and the pain. I heard his raspy voice as he came to realise that he wouldn't live to fight another day.

I slapped my palms against my forehead, as if trying to beat the image away, and groaned quietly. Grace reached out her hand and stroked my hair. Leaning forwards, she pressed her cool lips against my perspiring temple and told me everything was going to be alright.

It was a comfort to hear even though I knew that it wasn't true.

It wasn't going to be alright for Joaquin, was it?

We had had to leave Cuba as soon as possible. I felt wretched for leaving Catalina behind, but she promised she was going to be taken care of by her parents. She was moving back home.

I wished we could have stayed for the funeral, but Cuba was far too unstable for me to risk Grace's safety.

So, we left on the first possible flight.

I rummaged through my pockets until I found the Spanish dictionary I had bought before our trip. With my journal in hand, I painstakingly translated every word on the list until I knew what Joaquin's father had wanted his son to do before he died.

As I read through it, I knew I would keep my promise. We would finish it. Grace had always been desperate to experience life, to experience the world. Maybe this list would help us do that.

As the captain announced our descent, I knew exactly where we were going to go next.

"Where are we going?" Grace asked as I dragged her through the airport.

"Hurry, Gracie, or we'll miss the train," I replied, grabbing her bag and jogging.

"What? Jack, what are we missing? I can't run in these shoes."

I stopped and turned around, just as Grace bumped in to me, unprepared for my sudden halt. I gripped her shoulders to steady her and smiled. "Life, Gracie. Life."

She grinned and took my hand as I led her through the maze that was the airport, and out into the sun.

I could barely remember the details of the train ride. It passed by in a dim haze; my mind was focused on fulfilling the list buried in my coat pocket.

Grace sat beside me nervously, unsure of our destination, or our purpose. I had not yet told her about the list Joaquin had given me. I didn't want to upset her. Or perhaps I just didn't want to think about Joaquin for a second longer.

I let her take the window seat and, as we puttered along, she gasped at the scenery that passed. I watched it zoom by with a small smile on my face and rested into the journey.

If someone had asked me, just a year ago, where I thought my life would go, in my wildest dreams I never would have imagined that in January 1959,

I'd be trekking across Europe with my wife, preparing to take on Italy to finish a dead man's list.

Life is nothing if not full of surprises.

As I sat on the swaying train, watching with full appreciation as the snowy world passed me by, I realised something - something strange and unfamiliar. Though I felt a deep sorrow for Joaquin's untimely passing, a new revelation traipsed up and down my spine. It was a feeling that ravaged me, swimming through my veins and chewing on my bones. Pulsating under my skin, it refused to be ignored. I felt...I *was*...free.

This was an entirely new concept for me. As my head lolled back and forth with the train's sluggish and tired motions, I explored the new epicenter of my mind. My perspective had changed. Maybe I didn't have to find my identity in my pain anymore. But who did that leave me with?

I closed my eyes and leant my head back, attempting to acquaint myself with the stranger who had just moved into my mind's eye.

"Jack," Grace whispered, shaking me. "Jack."

My eyes opened as Grace snapped her fingers in front of my face. "Wakey-wakey," she cooed.

"What?" I mumbled, still half-asleep.

"You fell asleep. Get up. We're here." A broad smile filled her face and suddenly I was alert.

Italy. We had made it to Italy.

Getting off the train, I watched a hundred different emotions explode across Grace's face. Wonder, excitement, amazement, happiness.

"What's wrong?" I asked as I spotted something that looked like sadness flash across her features. She had been quick to hide it, masking it almost too fast for me to catch it.

"Nothing," she said, hoisting her bag over her shoulder.

"Gracie," I said in a disapproving tone.

She bit her bottom lip before sighing reluctantly. "It's just that I'm afraid," she said as if it didn't matter.

I took her hand in mine, reassuringly. "What of? Grace, Italy is nothing like Cuba, we're going to be safe here."

I hoped.

"No, I know. I've always wanted to come here, and I built it up so much in my mind that I'm afraid that it won't be what I had expected."

"Well, it won't be," I said matter-of-factly.

She looked at me and her face wrinkled with confusion at my blunt answer.

"Nothing is ever like we expected it to be. But give the country a chance to introduce itself to you and maybe it will be even better than you could have hoped for. Throw out your preconceptions and let the country speak for itself."

A small smile stretched across her lips and I knew in that moment there was a chance for us. A real chance that we would find happiness here, experience life here, just like she had always wanted to.

Her moment of illness in London was a fuzzy memory now; a fading black stain on the stretching white horizon. Maybe now there was hope, maybe now there was a future.

Chapter Nineteen

The list had told us to travel through Italy. That was exactly what we had been doing for the last two weeks.

As we puttered along the road in a hired car, I couldn't help but remember seeing Venice for the first time. I had never seen anything like it. Canals snaking through the buildings, beauty echoed everywhere you turned.

Taking our first ride in the long gondola was an experience I would never forget. We sailed around and, for once, time was on our side. We spent the day on the water and explored every facet of the city that we could.

I used almost a full roll of film snapping pictures of anything and everything that stood out.

As we sat on the gondola, swaying with the soft motion of the water, I pulled out my journal and began to write, describing what I could see to the best of my ability.

"What are you writing?" Grace asked, leaning over to inspect my humble, scribbled thoughts.

"Oh, nothing of any great consequence," I answered, suddenly feeling apprehensive. Grace was very well read, and my incoherent thoughts would probably appear childish to her.

"Can you read it to me?" she asked, resting her head on my shoulder.

"Uh, well..."

"Please?" She looked at me with those big brown eyes and I knew there was no way I could say no.

"Okay," I sighed. Slowly, I began to read.

20th January 1959

I sit in the gondola and watch the city of Venice float past. Italian songs are sung gently behind me by the gondolier. I cannot understand the words that flow melodically and naturally, but I feel I can understand their meaning. The gondolier smiles at Grace and points to the buildings, explaining their history in broken English. He seems to be just as in love with the city as I now am.

Wisps of light clouds cover the sun and there is a crisp chill in the air, but I do not feel its sting. People wave at us as they float past on gondolas of their own, some tourists and some local.

We smile and wave back, pretending for just a moment we're old friends, separated only by the water between us.

There is nothing but time in the city of Venice. As the oar pierces the skin of the water, propelling us forward, I cannot help but feel that there is some secret this city holds, sharing its poetry only with its inhabitants. A secret guarded, a secret withheld. A secret that would teach you how to truly live in every moment.

"It's beautiful," Grace said, entwining her fingers around mine.

I half smiled and snapped my book shut. "It's not finished yet."

"Jack," she said, not speaking again until I looked at her. "It's beautiful."

Grace was staring out the window as I drove down the empty road. Being January, the weather was icy cold, but that didn't matter so much to us. Everything was new and fresh and tinted in an awe-struck glow.

I had finally told Grace about the list when we spent three nights in Rome. I had joined her on the balcony, overlooking the ruins and the city landscape intertwining to create a melody of ancient and new.

"Grace, there's something I've been meaning to tell you," I said, looking away from the landscape and down to my hands.

"What is it?" she had asked.

"When we...on New Year's...when Joaquin..." I stuttered, unable to finish.

"Yes, I know, go on." Grace smiled softly, relieving me from finishing the horrid, unnatural sentence.

"Well, he gave something to me. Something that his father had given to him."

"Really?" she asked, straightening in her chair. "What is it?"

"A list."

She looked at me, confused. "A list? Of what?"

"Of things his father wanted him to do before he died. A list of things to do in life to make sure you're really living."

"Oh," she said. I watched the features of her face twist and I knew she was feeling a deep sense of loss and pain at the death of someone so young.

"Yeah. Uh, I translated it into English because he asked me, well, us, to finish it for him."

She was silent as I searched my pockets for the list. I handed her the folded piece of paper and she gently opened it up as if at any moment it might break, as if its existence was tied to the life of Joaquin and it was still unaware of his death.

She read the list and I watched as tears filled her eyes and dripped down her face. I reached out my hand for hers and tried to manage a smile.

"This is why we're in Italy?" she finally asked, looking up at me.

"Yeah. Yeah it is. I'm sorry that I didn't tell you earlier."

"That's okay, Jack," she answered. "That's okay."

I stared at the horizon and tried to force out the images of Joaquin's final moments, as Grace turned the list around in her hands.

"So," she said with forced brightness, "Where do we go next then?"

I looked over to her and smiled.

Chapter Twenty

It was March 1960 when I got the call. We were in Kyoto in Japan and I had never seen anything close to resembling the ancient ache of the city.

It was beautiful. We had arrived in Japan in early February and had only intended to stay for as long as it took to see the Geisha - number four on the list. We had seen the Geisha in the first week but couldn't bring ourselves to leave.

We were staying in a traditional apartment, with sliding papery doors and cherry blossoms outside. The pink flowers carpeted the ground like a thick blanket.

There weren't as many Geishas as there used to be and it was mainly tourists that they performed for. I felt sad that the ancient art was fading. Still, their grace was incredible. I had never seen tea carried out as though it were a sacred dance.

It was late afternoon, just before I got the call, that Grace and I went outside to watch the world fall asleep.

I sat down beside her and soaked up the day, happier than I had ever been before. I had everything I needed, everything I could want.

"Jack," Grace said as we sat looking over the backyard.

"Mmm," I responded, closing my eyes and leaning my head back.

"There's something I need to tell you." Her voice sounded unsure.

I snapped my head up and looked at her. "Gracie, what is it? Are you sick again? Do I need to call a doctor?" I got to my feet before she responded, about to dash into the house and call for help.

"No, no, no," she said, reassuringly. "Sit down, Jack. I'm fine."

"Oh." Relieved, I sat down again, knowing that whatever it was she had to say would be a hundred times better than hearing that she was sick again. I couldn't go through that, couldn't watch that pain. I didn't think I could survive.

"What is it?" I asked.

"It's... well, I..." she looked down at her hands and traced her finger along the lines of her palm.

"Gracie, you can tell me," I said, reaching my hands over and holding hers. "Just tell me."

"Okay," she said, letting out a big breath.

I leaned forward, looking at her face, trying to read her expression.

Nothing could prepare me for what she was about to say.

"I'm pregnant."

It was a long time before I said anything. The words took longer than I thought was possible to sink into my brain.

"Jack?" Grace said warily. "Are you okay?"

Her voice prompted me for a response.

"You're...pregnant?" I breathed.

"Yeah," she answered.

"You're pregnant," I repeated, more firmly this time.

"Yes," Grace said in the same tone.

I stood to my feet and stared at the backyard as the sun set and the sky grew dark. Slowly I turned around and looked at Grace's worried face.

"What!" I exploded, throwing my hands into the air.

"Jack!" Grace said, jumping back from my unexpected reaction.

"I...I...I can't even... oh man," I said, maintaining the same volume.

"Don't be mad, Jack," Grace said softly, looking down to the ground.

"What?" I shouted. "Mad? This is fantastic!" I laughed and pressed my palms against my head, shocked and amazed.

"What?" Grace asked, looking up at me. "It is?"

"Of course, it is! I'm going to be a father!" Suddenly I stopped and sat down. "Oh," my voice was quieter. "I'm going to be a....dad."

"Yeah," Grace said, touching her hand against my back.

"Grace," I said in a worried tone, looking up at her. "What if..."

"What if what, Jack?" she asked.

"What if I'm just like him?" My voice was pathetic and weak.

Grace shook her head and her mouth fell open. "Jack. How could you say that? You're nothing like him and you're not going to be anything like him. You're going to be an amazing father."

"Do you really think so?"

"I know so."

Grace leaned forward and kissed me, and I started to believe her.

It was an hour later that the phone rang. I bounded over to it, eager to tell whoever it was on the other end our good news, even if I didn't know them.

"Hello?" I answered excitedly.

"Jack? Jack, it's Frankie," came my brother's voice.

"Frankie!" I bellowed. "Oh, it's so good to hear from you. How are you?" I hardly recognised his voice. It was deeper, and he sounded more like an adult than I had expected.

"I'm fine, Jack. I-I..." he trailed off, his voice shaking ever so slightly.

"Frankie?" I spoke, all trace of excitement vanishing. Something was wrong. "What is it? Frankie, what's going on?"

"It's Dad," he whispered.

"What? What's happened? Frankie, spit it out."

"He's...he's had a heart attack."

There was silence. All of a sudden, I couldn't breathe.

"Jack? Are you there?" Frankie asked.

"Yeah," I breathed. "I'm here. Is he...alive?"

"Yes. He's in the hospital. I...I... I don't know what to do."

"I'll be there by tomorrow."

I hung up, threw some clothes in my bag, and went to find Grace.

Chapter Twenty-One

"Oh my..." Grace said when I told her about my father's heart attack. Her hand covered her mouth. "I'll just pack my bags."

"No," I said firmly, shaking my head.

"What?" She sounded horrified, offended.

"You can't come."

"Excuse me?" she spat at me. "Of course, I'm going to come!"

"No, Gracie, you're in the early months of your pregnancy. I don't want you flying and I don't want the stress of it on you and the baby."

"Jack! I can handle it! I'm coming!" She stamped her foot angrily.

"No, Grace. No."

Grace's mouth fell open in shock and fury. "How dare you tell me what to do?"

"Please," I said, weakly, too stunned to put up a fight. "Gracie, if...if anything happens to him, I can't handle the possibility of losing two people I love. Just...do this for me. Be safe for me. Keep that little one safe for me. Please."

Grace looked away from me and shook her head. "Fine. Emotional manipulation. Whatever, Jack."

I leaned forward and kissed her gently. I pulled away and pressed my forehead against hers. "Thank you. I love you."

As I went to walk away, Grace grabbed my wrist. I turned back to her as she put her hands on my cheeks and pulled my lips back to hers.

"I love you, too," she said sourly.

When I arrived at home, it was Frankie who picked me up at the airport.

"What are you doing driving?" I asked as I hopped into the passenger seat.

"Harry lets me, and they were busy, so I volunteered," Frankie answered in a voice so grownup I felt my chest constrict. He was only sixteen, but I felt like I had missed too much of his life already.

I reached across and hugged him tightly. "I've missed you," I said, pulling back.

"I've missed you too."

"How is he?" I asked.

"They said he's stable. I don't really know anything. It's... I got the call from the doctor who said my number was in his wallet and so was yours. He tried yours but, well, obviously it didn't work. There was no one at home – Robert was in hospital and I don't live there anymore."

"Yeah. Right. Have you been okay? How's everything going with Lou-Ellen and Harry?"

"It's great. Really. They treat me really well. I think, in a way, they kind of...need me. Harry can't do as much around the place as he used to, and Lou-Ellen likes my 'youthful spirit'. She says it keeps her young." Frankie chuckled, but the sound was tight.

I knew he was worried.

"What about you?" he asked. "How's life?" He laughed again, as if my life was such a mystery to him that the only logical response was laughter.

"Frankie, you would love Europe the most, I think. If you ever get the chance, you should go and see it. You could come back with me, you know," I said, staring out the window as we passed by the world that used to be so familiar to me. Now it felt strange, as if it had all just been a dream. "I promised you a trip to London."

We pulled up in front of the hospital and I hesitated before getting out of the car.

"What is it?" Frankie asked, his hand on the door handle.

"I, uh... I'm scared," I admitted, surprised at my own emotions and reluctance.

"Of what?" Frankie inquired.

"Losing him, I think. I wouldn't want things to end like this. Between us and him, I mean."

"I know," Frankie said tensely. "I've tried to forgive him, I really have. But it's hard. What he did to you, to me, it's...Anyway, I'm here and you're here and he's gonna be fine. He's going to live to hurt us another day. Let's go in."

I couldn't believe that this person was my little Frankie.

Frankie smiled at me reassuringly and got out of the car. I slowly followed, feeling unprepared for what I was about to face. A niggling voice in my mind kept reminding me to tell Frankie the update about Grace, but I didn't want to mar the sombre moment with my own selfish happiness.

I kept my mouth shut and walked into the hospital.

I followed Frankie, who seemed to know exactly where he was going. When we finally reached Robert's room, I stopped outside the closed door and Frankie stood motionless beside me.

I gripped his arm for support and felt my stomach heave and my chest constrict.

"Are you ready?" Frankie asked softly.

I didn't say anything, so Frankie didn't move. He stood beside me for excruciating minutes, waiting for me to come to terms with my father's condition.

"I'm ready," I finally breathed.

Frankie opened the door and walked inside. There, lying in the middle of the room, was Robert, my father.

His eyes were closed, with deep purple bruise-like marks above his cheekbones. He looked sallow and gaunt, with skin that almost looked yellow.

"Why-why is he that colour?" I asked.

"His liver is kickin' up a fuss," Frankie said, sitting down beside the bed and folding his arms across his chest.

"Oh," I said pathetically, lifting a hand to ruffle my hair.

"They say he'll be alright, though. At least, that's what they think."

I felt sick, like I was going to throw up. I couldn't bear looking at him in this condition. I pushed all of the anger and the pain that had been rooted inside me, to the back of my mind. He looked so alone, so broken. I had to forgive him; I had to let him know it was okay, in case...in case...I couldn't finish the thought.

"This sucks," I said weakly.

Frankie simply nodded, never taking his eyes from his father. "That it does."

I walked over to the sickly, pale green coloured wall and slid down until I landed on the floor. I put my elbows on my knees and waited.

Chapter Twenty-Two

I clutched my hand to my chest remembering that day. Lying flat on my back, looking up at the sky, I sucked in a deep breath as the memory swirled around my head.

I remembered the smell of the hospital, the smell of decaying lives and fading time. It was an all too familiar scene – my mother's passing, my father's pain.

It never ceased to amaze me, the turns that life can throw. Its ability to completely derail its captive passengers and tilt them off balance makes each day a precarious and tentative walk along the tight rope of time.

I lifted my hands and stared at them above my head. Thick fingers that used to be nimble and clever, wrinkles in the place of what was once smooth skin, scars accumulated over a lifetime of wear.

Nothing ever stayed the same. Time spent was time that could never be retrieved. I had spent a lot of my life wondering if I had spent my time well. I was often plagued with the fear that I could have been better. Had I been enough? Was my life insufficient? Did I not deserve my space here on earth?

It was only in the last few years, when I had already reached the winter of my life, and spent the spring, summer and autumn fighting to be enough, that I realised that being enough is the wrong aim. For who can ever say what enough truly is?

Is not a man who works as a garbage collector, but loves and loves well, equal to a man who, in the eyes of the world, is greater because he has built a monetary empire? What is best to achieve from life? Who decides what is success and what is failure?

There was nothing at all I could do about the time I had already spent. I could only affect the time that was to come. At that moment, on the hospital floor, I was afraid of the time to come. I was afraid of the man the years would shape me into. Would I be just like the man in front of me? Or was I just different enough to realise that I didn't have to follow in his footsteps. Could I let it go?

The soft murmur of voices stirred me from the slumber I hadn't realised I had entered. The first thing I noticed was that moonlight was pouring in from the hospital windows, mixing with the yellow glow of streetlights to form a pattern on the ground.

The next thing I noticed was Frankie sitting on the side of my father's bed, looking down at his hands as Robert spoke to him in a raspy voice.

I sat there, still and unmoving, not wanting to disturb them. Suddenly Frankie stood up from the bed and turned to face me. I saw his face was wet with tears and his eyes were dark and bloodshot.

He didn't say a word, so I didn't dare speak. He simply nodded in my direction and left the room.

Robert watched him leave and then turned to face me.

"I guess that means it's your turn," he said, coughing to clear his throat.

I stood up and walked over to his side. "Is Frankie okay?" I asked.

"I think he'll be alright," he replied, not meeting my eyes.

"What's going on?" I asked. "Did you get some test results back or something?"

"No, no," Robert said, taking deep breaths in after every few words. "I just had to have a little talk with him."

"About what?" I asked, crossly. Frankie looked upset and I wasn't sure if I could retain my composure if Robert had abused Frankie while lying in a hospital bed on the cusp of death.

"About...me, I suppose. About how poorly I treated him."

"Oh," I said, dropping into the chair beside the bed.

"Yeah. I've had a lot of time to think about what I've done. Seeing as how I'm not looking too good, right now, I thought there's no time like the present to try and set things right."

"Okay." I watched his pale figure, accented by the silver slices of moonlight, gently rise and fall with every breath. He already looked like a ghost.

"I said I was sorry for letting him get taken away. That was... well, anyway. He's been better off, so I'm glad in a way that I lost him. It gave him a chance, you know?"

I nodded weakly.

"He, uh, he's been pretty angry with me." He heaved in a breath and coughed violently. "Can't say I blame him, though, really. Guess I've been pretty mad at myself, too."

"Does he...forgive you?"

"I don't know. Maybe one day he will, though it's more than I deserve. Isn't it?"

The question was rhetorical, but I couldn't help but feel he was asking himself, more than he was asking me.

"So, now, it's your turn. I...I...I've treated you worse than anyone. I've hit you. There is no circumstance that makes that okay. I've made you pick up after me and take care of your brother and run that stupid garage without me. I've been selfish. Real selfish. I..." Robert paused and then breathed out agonising sobs. Tears dripped from his eyes and ran down his weathered face. "I am s-sorry, son. I'm so sorry."

I never thought I would see him cry tears other than those he shed for my mother.

Robert raised a hand to cover his eyes and wept. "I'm sorry, I'm sorry," he mumbled, over and over again.

I couldn't bear it. I moved to sit on the side of his bed and leant forward, wrapping my arms around him. The tears that drenched my shirt fought to wash away the years of pain he had caused, as this proud man crumbled into nothing in my arms.

Then I did the most powerful and horrific thing I could.

I forgave him. For everything.

Chapter Twenty-Three

I was back. In my old home. I had spent the night on the hospital floor and now I found myself wandering the halls of my childhood home alone. Stopping at the door of my old bedroom, I peered inside and saw nothing at all had changed. Time had forgotten this room, overlooked the walls that had muffled the angry shouts of a hurt teenager, the pillow that had absorbed my tears and the closet that contained barely anything but oil stained work shirts.

It felt strange. Almost as though this room was too small for me now, like I didn't fit. I was too big. Like the boy that used to live here had nothing to do with the man that I had become.

I walked inside and sat down on the springy bed. I leant back until I was staring at the ceiling and put my feet up. How many hours I had spent lying here and dreaming of another world, another life in which I was free, happy.

In all my years of dreaming, I never actually thought I'd get it.

There was nothing I wanted more than to leave this town behind and sail into a new world, a new reality. I could hardly believe I had actually succeeded.

"Jack?" I heard an old familiar voice call.

I sat up and left the room, heading out to where the voice had come from. "Lou-Ellen!" I called when I saw my brother's guardian standing in my kitchen beside Harry and Frankie. "What are you doing here?"

"Well, we couldn't leave you boys to fend for yourselves here while your father's in hospital, so we thought we would come and lend a hand." Lou-

Ellen pulled me close and hugged me tightly. I hadn't realised I had missed her.

"Well, it's so good to see you," I said when she let me go.

"Yes, though it would be better if it was under different circumstances." She pursed her lips thoughtfully and patted my cheek before she turned around and looked at the kitchen. "Right! First thing's first. Food."

We spent the afternoon cooking and eating. Lou-Ellen was talented in the kitchen and made a dozen things I had never tried before. All were culinary masterpieces.

There was a sense of family wherever Lou-Ellen and Harry were and I was so grateful that they had been the ones to take Frankie in. He was so much better for it.

As the sun began to set, Frankie and Harry left to take Robert a few odds and ends, such as books and pictures, that might make his stay in the hospital more comfortable. Lou-Ellen and I stayed behind to clean up.

"So," Lou-Ellen said, eyeing me with a knowing stare. "How are you holding up?"

"Uh, I don't know, to be honest," I said, drying the dishes she washed. "It's kind of strange. I mean, I feel strange."

"That's to be expected, my dear."

"I just... it all feels wrong, being back here. I don't know what to do or what to think. I... I want to go home. Is that wrong? I don't know what to do Lou-Ellen."

"*Be sure you put your feet in the right place, then stand firm.* Abraham Lincoln said that. If your feet are in the right spot, Jack, my boy, then stand there, stay there and refuse to be moved. You cannot live your life for others."

"But who is going to take care of him when he's out of the hospital?"

"Who is going to take care of you, and everything you have to get back to, if not you? Haven't you spent too many years already taking care of your father? Besides, Harry and I have already talked about it with Frankie and we're bringing Robert home with us when the doctors say he can go. It shouldn't be longer than a month after that until he is back on his feet."

I stared at Lou-Ellen, completely speechless. If there was anyone living on earth that I wanted to resemble, it was her. I couldn't have asked for a better role model.

Four weeks later, having endured the insufferable pain of being without Grace on a daily basis, I was sitting on the edge of the lounge chair listening to Frankie and his girlfriend, Katherine, talk about how they met.

"Frankie was very heroic. He stood up for me." Katherine, or Kate as she preferred to be called, sat beside Frankie with a shy smile on her face. Her dark red hair was tied up out of her face and Frankie was staring at her with adoration.

"No, not really," Frankie said, waving his hand. "Those guys were just out of line. I did what anyone in their right mind would have."

Apparently, Frankie had rescued Kate from the clutches of six or so school bullies. It was love at first sight.

I chuckled to myself as I watched them chatting and laughing. I wished Grace was here. It had been so long since I had seen her. Long weeks of waiting, working in the garage and waiting some more had passed by at the slowest pace imaginable.

Robert was still in the hospital, slowly recovering. We visited him every day, bringing him his favourite foods and anything we found that might encourage him as he waited for his body to heal.

It was good to spend time with him without the influence of alcohol purging every good thing from his system, and seeing Frankie every day reminded me of just how much I missed him.

To be back working in the garage was a peculiar experience. I slipped back into the ebb and flow of my old life and eventually I began to wonder if the new life I had come to know was just a dream.

"Jack! Frankie!" I heard the front door open and Lou-Ellen called out to us.

"We're in the living room, Lou-Ellen," Kate called out in a happy voice.

"Ah, Kate," Lou-Ellen said as she leaned around the corner. "Lovely to see you, my dear. Guess what, boys? I have an excellent surprise."

"What is it?" Frankie asked.

"I just got back from the hospital. Your father is able to come home at the end of the week!" Lou-Ellen smiled happily and clapped her hands together.

I sighed deeply, relieved. That meant he was out of harm's way. He was going to be alright. He wasn't going to die.

And I would be able to go home.

"You could come visit me soon, you know," I said to Frankie as I hugged him goodbye at the airport.

"I can't, Jack," he said. "Dad needs me."

"Yeah, of course. But if you change your mind..."

"Lou-Ellen and Harry would be lost without me. Besides, you know, Kate would miss me too much," Frankie chuckled sheepishly.

"Mmm, yes, Katherine, the girlfriend. She was nice."

"Yeah, she's great, isn't she?" Frankie smiled.

"You take care, hey? I miss you."

Frankie buried his head in my chest again. "I miss you too, Jack."

I hugged Harry and shook his hand, then turned to Lou-Ellen, trying to find the words to thank her for everything she had done for me.

"I..." was all I could say.

Lou-Ellen pulled me close and slapped my back softly. "Fly safe, my dear. Don't you worry about anything back here. Go on. Live."

I watched them disappear into the sea of Taxis and busses. Finally, I turned around and headed for my plane.

I had plenty of time to think over my last conversation with Robert before I left. I had sat beside him and held his rough, tired hands, wishing I had something good to say. I couldn't think of anything at all.

"You be safe, then, boy," Robert said, patting my shoulder weakly.

"I will," I answered. I decided to throw caution to the wind and hugged him. It was getting easier. More natural.

"Bye, Jack."

"Bye...Dad."

I stood and walked to the door, pausing briefly at the threshold. I cleared my throat and forced the words to come. "You do deserve to be forgiven. I...I forgive you."

Robert's mouth popped open and I saw tears fill his eyes. He coughed and nodded, looking away, unable to keep eye contact with me.

I left the room and had no idea when I would see him again. But, maybe, just maybe, there was a chance we could somehow have a relationship in the future.

As the captain announced our imminent landing, I quelled the butterflies in my stomach. I was desperate to get back to my wife and unborn child.

I moved as quickly as I could off the plane and through the lines to collect my baggage. It felt like years had passed before I finally stepped outside into a sunny Japanese day. Grace and I were going to fly back to London as soon as I was less terrified about her flying.

A beautiful woman caught my attention and I dropped my bags and ran to her, unable to resist picking her up and swirling her around in my arms.

Grace laughed in my ear and kissed my cheek. "I missed you too," she said when I stopped and put her down.

"What are you doing here?" I asked, cutting myself off to bend down and kiss her. "I thought I was getting a Taxi."

"On your first overseas adventure without me, did you think I would make you catch a Taxi home? Please."

"Oh, I've missed you so much." I bent down and looked straight at her stomach. "Hello little buddy. I've missed you too. Did you take care of Mummy?"

Grace laughed and slapped my head. "Stop it!" She looked around, embarrassed.

"I love you, Gracie," I said, standing up to hug her tightly.

"Jack, you have no idea."

Chapter Twenty-Four

It was perhaps the most surreal experience of my life. Grace was in more pain than I could have imagined, but somehow, it was a peaceful pain, because she knew, at the end of the seemingly unending agony, she would have a child.

A small little piece of her and me would enter the world, wrapped in the fragile form of a baby. Another life we were entirely responsible for.

On this, the fourteenth of October 1960, I was going to become a father.

I was petrified.

I held Grace's hand and watched beads of sweat appear on her forehead. Tears were in her eyes and I knew she was expelling more energy than she had.

"It's okay," I whispered, unsure what to say or do.

Grace screamed, and the sound was deafening. I could hardly bear it.

The doctor stood in front of her, encouraging her and giving instructions. I couldn't look away from her face. I had to know she was alright.

"Congratulations," the doctor said when Grace's face relaxed ever so slightly.

Suddenly I could hear the sound of a baby crying and I knew that it was over. I was a father.

"You are now the proud parents," the doctor continued.

I held my breath.

"Of a baby boy." My mouth dropped open as I turned to look at the doctor who held a blood covered child in his hands.

"I have a son," I breathed, disbelieving.

"You have a son," Grace confirmed in a breathless, ecstatic voice.

"I can't believe it!" I bent down and kissed Grace on the cheek, completely in awe.

Once the baby had been taken away to be washed and clothed, a nurse returned with my son in her arms. She placed him gently in my care. His soft face and scrunched nose was tinted pink and his hands were so small. I was instantly terrified I was going to break him.

"It's okay," the nurse said softly. "He's tough. Don't worry."

I looked at her with furrowed brows, completely unsure. I bent down to Grace, so she could see the result of her pain. I gently placed our son in her arms and watched tears drip down her face. The child nestled into her and I couldn't believe how fortunate I was.

I was utterly terrified. And loving every moment.

"What should we call him, Gracie?" I asked, brushing her sweaty hair back out of her face.

"I don't know," she said, letting out a breath of a laugh, "I can't think straight at the moment."

"How about Charles? Or David?" I wondered aloud, knowing immediately they were wrong.

"No," Grace said. "What about..."

"Christopher," I said, finishing her sentence.

"Christopher. I love it. Little Chris."

I sat down on the chair beside the bed and leant against Grace's arm. I loved them desperately.

My family.

My wife and my son, Christopher.

Chapter Twenty-Five

I bolted upright in bed. Someone was crying. Who? Why? Half asleep, I threw the covers from my legs and stood on shaky feet. "What's going on?" I mumbled.

I looked around and noticed Grace wasn't lying down beside me.

For one brief second, I panicked. But when I heard Grace cooing softly, my mind relaxed and I remembered something I was still getting used to. I was a father now. And babies tend to cry in the middle of the night.

I bent down and flicked on the bedside light behind me. A warm yellow glow filled the room and I rubbed my eyes fiercely as they tried to adjust.

Leaving the room, I tiptoed down the hall and stopped at the nursery. The walls were painted soft sky blue and the cot in the middle was a pale custard yellow. I had never worked harder on anything than I had on that cot. I was afraid it was going to fall down in the middle of the night. I couldn't bear the thought and I was sure nothing in the history of the world was more secure than that cot.

Stuffed toys lined the window sill and in the corner of the room was a rocking chair. I peered around the corner and leant against the door frame. Sitting in the chair was Grace, her wavy dark hair dripping down past her left shoulder, with the tiny child I loved so much squirming in her arms.

I watched as Grace wiped a tear from Christopher's face. With one last gurgle of noise, Christopher closed his eyes and went to sleep, calm in his mother's arms.

Grace swayed gently in the chair humming softly and I smiled, all traces of tiredness replaced with contentment and peace.

"Hey," Grace whispered, spotting me at the door.

"Hi," I replied, looking into her serene face.

"What are you doing? Are you okay?" she asked.

"Yeah. Hey, let me take over. You go back to sleep."

"Are you sure?" she asked sleepily.

"Absolutely. Pass him here."

Grace stood from the chair and gently placed him in my arms, before kissing my cheek and brushing back my hair. "I love you."

"You have no idea," I answered, stepping forward to take her place in the rocking chair.

Grace paused at the door and looked back to us. "I like this," she said.

"What do you like?"

"This. You, me, Christopher. I like this." She smiled and turned to walk down the hall towards the rest of the night's sleep.

"Me too," I whispered to myself, looking down at my son. "Me too."

I wasn't sure why, but I had never expected to be a father. It didn't seem like something that would happen for me. But now that I sat here, with a tiny life in my hands, I couldn't imagine living any other way.

I held a person in my arms; someone with a future, who would have hopes and dreams and aspirations. He would grow up to be a banker or a lawyer or a doctor or whatever his heart desired, and this is where it all began. Right here. Sitting in a rocking chair with his father – a moment he would never remember, and a memory I would never forget.

"I love you, little Christopher," I whispered, looking over his sleeping face.

The fear had not yet left my side. It had bludgeoned me every day for the last two weeks – since Christopher was born. Would I turn out to be just like my father?

I prayed that I wouldn't. There was nothing in the world I wanted more than to protect this tiny child in my arms. But could I beat genetics? Could I find a way to be better than just a product of my upbringing?

I wanted to be his hero. I wanted to be a real father. The trouble was that I had no one to look to for an example. I sat in the rocking chair, watching my son sleeping, terrified that I wouldn't raise him as well as he deserved.

When I thought about it, I had no idea how to look after a child. I was still a child myself in so many ways. This person relied on me and Grace was counting on me to be a good father to him. I couldn't let them down. But there was no manual, there were no instructions. I was a million miles from my hometown, in a city that I loved, but had no real connections in, stranded in fatherhood.

I found myself wishing my mother was here. Not a day went by that I didn't think of her and I had never wished that I could see her face, feel her comforting embrace or hear her words of encouragement, more than I did at that moment.

I cleared my throat and fought against the rising lump threatening to choke me. I was completely overwhelmed. In thirty seconds, I had managed to convince myself I was useless, and I was going to fail.

I'm going to be the worst father in the world, I thought to myself. My mind was racing, and my stomach rolled with uncertainty.

Please God, I prayed silently. *Please, please, please.* I didn't have anything else to say. I couldn't form the thoughts or the words, couldn't express my fear and anxiety. I just hoped that 'please' was all God needed to hear.

I placed my hand against Christopher's chest and relaxed slightly in the chair. I leant back and stared at the ceiling when I felt something touch my finger. Christopher had lifted a hand and grabbed my finger, squeezing it with all the strength his tiny hand could muster.

I looked down and straight into the deep brown eyes of my son, who stared at me, holding my hand. I hadn't even realised he had woken up. He didn't make a sound. For countless moments, he just rested in my arms and looked up at me. I saw nothing but pure love in his eyes and suddenly the fluttering butterflies calmed, and I knew that I would be alright.

It wasn't written in stone. I decided who I wanted to be. Not my past.

I was going to give my son everything I could. I was going to be a good father and I was not going to let him down.

I pushed out whatever was left of my fearful thoughts and reveled in the unspoken conversation I shared with my son until our eyes grew heavy and we both fell asleep.

Chapter Twenty-Six

"He's two years old, Jack, not two days! He'll be fine for a trip to Australia," Grace exclaimed, shaking her head at me as if I was being completely unreasonable. It was early in 1963 and Grace was adamant we take another trip. I however, was not.

"But what if something happens, Grace? What if something horrible and unforeseen puts him in danger!" I protested.

"Jack, you're being completely ridiculous! Besides, we haven't touched Joaquin's list since he was born. Come on, you know it's next. It's Australia, not Mount Vesuvius! Don't you want to dive in the Barrier Reef?"

"Of course, I want to go, but, but..." I realised I didn't really have an argument. I was just being overprotective.

"Stralia," I heard Christopher attempt to speak.

"See, Jack? Chris wants to go, too. There's nothing to worry about!"

I dropped down on the chair at the kitchen table and watched Grace stretch her lips into a pleading smile.

"Fine," I grumbled. "We'll go."

"Thank you," Grace replied, kissing me quickly before she scooped Christopher off and danced down the hall, humming happily.

"Sharks!" I shouted suddenly, calling after her. "What about sharks!"

The plane touched down on Australian soil and despite my reservations for my son's safety, I was excited to be travelling again. We hadn't been anywhere since Christopher was born, not even back to my hometown to introduce him to my family. I had been far too concerned about the effects of high altitude on a baby. Apparently, there was nothing to worry about – Chris looked ecstatic.

The first thing I noticed was the climate. It was muggy, and the air was so thick I was almost swimming across the tarmac instead of walking. Four hours later, I was freezing cold.

The second thing I noticed was that we were definitely not in London anymore. I fell in love with the country instantly. We had arrived at Melbourne airport and had caught a Taxi to our hotel. Number fourteen on the list was to swim in the Great Barrier Reef and number twelve was to go on a long road-trip. Grace decided we would combine the two and drive from Melbourne to Airlie Beach, from which we could get to the reef. I had tried to convince her that Australia was much bigger than England and we would be travelling approximately two and a half thousand kilometers, but she was excited, and I couldn't disappoint her.

Grace and I talked more in the week we took to get to Airlie Beach than we had in a long time. I found that I missed her, even though we were living in the same house.

Life has a way of distracting you, dragging you onto a road that, before you know it, has engulfed you. We had become settled in a routine, in a pattern, and that meant we crossed paths without ever really seeing each other.

Having a young son took up so much of our time, but it was not parenthood that had done it to us. It was simply that we had become comfortable with the norm and had forgotten that life is an adventure meant to be lived and experienced.

We had been so sure that our lives would never be made up of the hum drum, the constant, the normal. Yet, somehow, we had been absorbed into it without ever having noticed. Life could be whatever we made it, and I missed making it exciting.

There was no rule saying life had to be made up of a nine to five job or confined to the restrictions of cynical thought. Every day was a choice, and I decided in that moment, that my choice was to make sure my family knew exactly how to get the most out of their lives.

"What are you thinking about?" Grace asked me.

"You," I answered with a cheeky grin.

She smiled, pushed up her sunglasses, and looked back to the barren road ahead. "Good answer."

The coral was electric - bright in its natural glory. It was an incredible experience. The world's biggest reef was not a disappointment. The sunburn I received, however, was. It turned out that floating on your stomach with your bare back to the Australian sky caused unimaginable pain later.

Even so, it was worth it.

Grace and I had kept Christopher afloat and watched him giggle and cackle with glee at the fish that swam past him. He threw out his hands, trying to clutch onto the colourful tails that swept past him.

His face lit up with a mixture of joy and terror when a fish as big as I was sailed past him. He threw his arms around Grace's neck and squealed with delight.

"I told you this would be fun," Grace said to me, when we came up for air.

"I know, I know," I answered, slapping Christopher's hands against the water. There was nothing better than the sound of him giggling as the water splashed all over his face.

"I've really missed this," Grace said, echoing the thoughts I had earlier. She turned to float on her back and closed her eyes against the bright sun.

"Hey, Grace," I called.

She looked across to me and raised an eyebrow.

"Thanks. Thanks for making us come."

Grace smiled and turned back to the sky, floating along in the water. "I know what's best for my boys."

I laughed. "Yes, you certainly do."

Chapter Twenty-Seven

I dropped the phone and heard it clamour against the floor.

"Jack, what was that?" I heard Grace call from the other room. She was still unpacking her suitcase from our Australian adventure.

After a few seconds of blinking blindly at the wall, trying to come to terms with what I had just heard, I bent down and picked up the phone, fumbling with it and nearly dropping it again as I tried to bring it back to my ear.

"What?" I yelled into the phone.

"I said, I'm getting married."

"I...I...I..." I was speechless.

"Jack?" the voice on the phone shouted, trying to get my attention.

"You....Frankie...my little brother...you're getting....married?!" I could hardly form the words.

"Yes!" Frankie shouted in response, his throaty laughter echoing in my ears.

"Oh...congratulations little brother!" I said, running my fingers through my hair, hardly coming to terms with the fact that my little brother, my little Frankie, had just called to tell me he was engaged.

"Thanks, Jack. Thanks," Frankie said sheepishly.

This felt so strange. I had missed so much of Frankie's life. It killed me inside. He had just turned nineteen. Of course, he could get married. He was an adult.

Time had gone past so quickly, and I wasn't sure why I found it so difficult to understand that my brother hadn't been left behind by the hand of time. I felt my chest tighten, thinking of all the moments of his life that I hadn't been there for. Birthdays, graduation and other milestones had passed without me. I had tried to come back for his graduation, but it was just at the time that Christopher became ill and I couldn't leave Grace alone to deal with it.

"Well, who's the lucky one, then? Is it Katherine?" I asked, mentioning the only girl I had ever heard him speak of.

"Yeah, it's Kate. She's really excited. I asked her earlier yesterday. I would have called you as soon as she said yes, but you probably wouldn't have appreciated a call in the middle of the night!"

"I wouldn't have minded for information like this! I can't even...this is just... I'm so proud of you!"

"Thanks, Jack," Frankie said. I could hear the smile in his voice.

I leant back against the wall and slid down until I was on the floor, the phone held under my chin.

"What's going on?" Grace asked, popping her head into the room.

"Frankie's getting married," I mouthed to her as Frankie babbled on about how excited he was.

Grace's eyes grew wide, before she threw her fist into the air and danced away.

"So, when's the big day?" I asked.

"July thirteenth," he replied happily.

"July thirteenth," I repeated, amazed. "What has Robert said about all this?"

"Oh, I don't know. I haven't told him yet."

"Frankie," I said in a disapproving tone. "You have to tell him."

"I will, I will, don't worry! I thought I owed it to you, you know? I wanted you to know before him."

"Thanks, Frankie. Are Lou-Ellen and Harry over the moon?"

"Lou-Ellen is so excited she hasn't stopped talking about it. She loves Kate. She says that of course she knew it was coming – it was only a matter of time. Harry keeps going on about what it takes to be a husband."

"Well, it takes a lot. But it's pretty amazing when you get the right person, little brother."

"Yeah, that's what I thought. Kate's the right one. I know she is."

"Well, I expect to see an invitation in the mail very soon." I twisted the phone cord in my fingers wondering what it was going to feel like to see my little brother get married.

Frankie chuckled. "Well, you are going to be my best man, so an invitation would probably help."

Chapter Twenty-Eight

"I can't believe this!" Grace yelled, walking into our room with a frustrated look on her face.

"What?" I asked, wondering what horrible thing could have happened in the last twenty minutes.

"I can't go!" she said, crossing her arms angrily.

"What do you mean? To Frankie's wedding? Gracie, the tickets are booked, we're leaving tomorrow!"

"Yeah, well, I guess I'm going to have to get a refund," she snapped.

"Gracie, tell me what you mean. I'm not following."

Grace looked at me and glowered. "I'm pregnant."

I shot up from where I was seated on the side of the bed and stared at her in disbelief. "What?"

"I'm pregnant." Suddenly a huge grin spread across her face and her eyes lit up. "We're having another baby."

"Oh, Gracie! That is unbelievable!" I shouted, running around to hug her.

"Well, yes, but I'm so mad. I can't go! You won't let me fly in my first trimester!"

I sighed disappointedly. "Great," I grumbled sarcastically.

"I'm so disappointed. I won't be able to see Frankie get married. I was so looking forward to it!"

"I know," I said as she rested her head on my shoulder. "I know."

Frankie had said that the chapel had been decorated according to Kate's taste. I wasn't surprised, given yellow roses didn't scream 'Frankie'. He didn't seem to mind at all.

"I wish she was here," Frankie said.

I didn't have to wonder who he meant. He was talking about our mother.

"I know," I answered. "She would be so proud, little brother."

"Do you think," Frankie asked, pausing briefly. "Do you think she would like Kate?"

"No," I said shaking my head. "I know she would love her."

Frankie smiled and patted his pocket where the aging picture of our mother was sitting. It was his way of involving her in his day.

Moments of silence passed and as I retied his bowtie and ruffled his hair until it sat more naturally atop his head, he gripped my shoulders and sucked in a deep and terrified breath as if someone had just wounded him.

"Frankie?" I stared into his eyes, wondering if he was going to pass out. What had gone wrong in the last thirty seconds?

"I'm getting married," he said in a whisper, as if this was news to him.

"Yes. I know. Are you alright?" I asked, resisting the urge to check his pulse. "Frankie!" I snapped my fingers in front of his eyes.

"Married!" His face was blank.

"Yes. Married. Frankie, are you okay? Can you do this? We have to go in two minutes!"

I was nervous now. He looked completely shocked, as if he hadn't been present when he proposed. Was he going to go through with it? Was he going to leave Kate at the altar? "Make up your mind. Right now!"

"I can't," he said, looking at the ground.

My stomach sank. I couldn't say a word. Already my mind was thinking through the next steps I would have to take. Explaining everything to Kate, her family and the waiting congregation was not going to be a pleasant experience.

"I can't..." Frankie said again, "believe I'm this lucky."

"What?" I said, surprised.

"Kate, that woman out there," Frankie sighed, gesturing to the church hall behind the doors, "picked me. Me. How did that happen? I don't deserve her."

I let out a deep sigh, utterly relieved. "Come on, Frankie," I said, chuckling. "You don't want to be late for your own wedding, do you?"

Standing beside my brother at the altar, I couldn't help but think back to my own wedding. The joy I felt, the peace that filled me. I couldn't believe I could be that lucky, either.

As the back door to the church creaked open, I slapped Frankie's back gently and smiled. My little brother, my little Frankie, was grown. He was getting married.

Time ticks by at supersonic speed, leaving you behind if you don't learn to run the race alongside it. Quite often the most treasured of moments are the unsuspecting joys you didn't even think to pay close attention to. It is then, at the end of your life, that you look back on those moments and wish you were there, truly present and accounted for.

I had missed so many of those moments of my brother's life and I couldn't have been more grateful that at least I had made it home for what would be one of the biggest moments of his life.

I wasn't going to miss a second of this day.

A familiar figure sat in the front row. He looked aged and gaunt, but his eyes were clear. His hair was flecked with dozens of silver strands and his skin had crinkled like paper. Robert twisted his hands in his lap and then fought with the tie of his suit. I smiled at him as he looked up and saw my stare. He nodded and smiled in return.

It had been a long road, and there was still a long road ahead, but we were getting somewhere, I knew we were. Slowly, brick by brick, piece by piece, we were rebuilding the relationship that had been abandoned and turned to rubble long ago.

As the bridesmaids finished their walk and the music swelled, I turned my eyes from the congregation. The guests had their eyes glued to the back door, but I wanted to see something else. I kept my eyes on Frankie.

I wanted to see his reaction when his bride walked inside.

Frankie didn't disappoint.

He didn't smile or cry. He just stared at the love of his life with a serene look of adoration. His face was smooth and sure, and his eyes were soft and loving.

He was making the right decision. I was sure of it.

Frankie took Kate's hands and the couple stood facing each other. She looked lovely, with her red hair intricately tied up, and a white dress that softly draped to the floor.

The preacher began to speak and, before I knew it, Frankie was saying "I do."

Then, the husband and wife kissed each other to the chorus of claps and shouts of congratulations from the guests.

I smiled as I watched Frankie walk down the aisle with his wife's arm in his and wished that my Gracie was by my side.

Chapter Twenty-Nine

Her name was Evelyn. My great aunt would have been appalled that I had decided to name my daughter after her, claiming it didn't need to be done, but I wanted to. After all, Evelyn had given us so much. She had helped us to live the life we had wanted to.

More than once, I found myself heading out at obscene hours of the night to bring home salmon, yoghurt or pickles, to satisfy Grace's peculiar cravings.

When she was five months pregnant, I made seven trips in one night. Every time I brought something home, she would shake her head and complain, giving me a new list of items to bring home until, by the time I returned from the seventh trip, the kitchen was a mess and she was fast asleep.

None of that bothered me, now that I stood in the nursery, holding my baby girl in my arms. She was so small, so delicate. I couldn't believe that she had come from me. I bent down and kissed her cheek and swayed her back and forth in my arms.

Just as I managed to get her to sleep, an ear-splitting wail filled my ears, waking Evelyn, who immediately began to cry.

I left the nursery and walked into the living room, where Grace was holding Christopher in her arms, trying to calm him down.

"What happened, Gracie?" I asked.

"He tripped," she said, sounding flustered.

"Here, let's swap." I stepped forward and we traded children.

Grace left the room and cooed Evelyn into silence.

"Hey buddy," I said, putting Christopher on the ground. "What happened?" I crouched down until I was almost his height. "Are you alright?"

Christopher rubbed his eyes, his lower lip trembling. "No," he mumbled.

"You know what I think would make you feel better?" I asked, grinning.

"What?" Christopher lowered his hands and eyed me curiously.

"A trip to Big Ben!" I said, sounding overly excited.

Christopher's eyes grew wide and he smiled. "Yes!" he shouted.

Pleased at my success, having bribed my son into a happier mood, I scooped him up onto my shoulders and told Grace where we were going.

It was nice to spend time with my son, and a trip to see Big Ben was easily accomplished. Christopher loved it. He asked to see it at least once a week, and I had no idea what his fascination with the clock tower was. There were so many things to see and do in London, but it was only ever Big Ben that he wanted to see.

We left the house, Chris still on my shoulders, and trekked down the road. We didn't live far from Big Ben, only a ten-minute walk.

As I settled into a smooth pace, I couldn't help but marvel at how we had come to be here. This life seemed so far removed from the life I had known before. I didn't deserve it. I had never expected to be a husband, a father, an adult.

Or truly happy, for that matter.

I had never felt such a weight of responsibility on my shoulders before. Even having to raise Frankie and take care of the shop paled into insignificance compared to the overpowering truth that I was a father. I had two young people who relied on me, who needed me, and I had to be there, every time.

It was exhausting, but I wouldn't have changed it for the world. I found that I needed my children just as much as they needed me. I couldn't imagine living without them.

Christopher slapped my head and squealed.

"Ladies and gentlemen, this is your Captain speaking," I said in a husky voice. "We have now arrived at our destination. As you can see, Big Ben hasn't changed a bit since our last visit."

Christopher laughed and pointed up to the large hands on the clock face.

"Look! Look!" he said. "It moved!"

I took another step forward and looked up at the clock. I wished, in that moment, that I could see what my son could see.

He was content just to be, to stare at a clock and marvel. The smallest things pleased him, and I wished I could be more like him.

Why, when we crossed into the realm of adulthood, did we forget how to love and live like children? When did concerning ourselves with the difficulties of life become the accepted thing to do? Whatever happened to simple happiness?

I wanted to view the world with the peace and simplicity that my son did.

Chapter Thirty

By the time Evelyn was thirteen, we had crossed twenty-three things off the list Joaquin had given me. Every time I dug out the old scrap of paper and pondered our next trip, I thought of him and the life that had been taken away.

I could still see Catalina's tear-streaked face in my mind and I wished more than anything I could reach into the past and change what had happened that New Year's Eve in 1958.

As I sat in my study, surrounded by copies of the photos I had taken and sold to newspapers, magazines and art galleries, I fingered the paper in my hands and pondered that fateful night, eighteen years ago.

I was a thirty-eight-year-old man and the memory still brought tears to my eyes.

I could hear Catalina screaming, the sounds of her pain drumming into my head. Was I to blame? Was there more I could have done? If I had been paying more attention, maybe it wouldn't have happened, maybe Joaquin would still be alive.

Catalina was out there somewhere, still feeling the hollow, bitter ache of loss. Perhaps her life was whole and full. Perhaps she was smiling and laughing and living every day to the best of her ability. But I knew, in the quiet moments, her memories would creep up on her like a shadowed thief and remind her of her loss. Her heart would thunder violently when the crack in her reality haunted her dreams.

I wasn't really sure if I believed anyone could ever get over a loss like that.

People move on and grow and change and learn to live again, but the wound has been inflicted and the scar will ever remain.

Occasions pass, and their memory is dragged to the forefront of the mind, tainting the moments meant to be held most dear.

Can one ever reverse the love they held for someone before they were taken from their lives? It is not always anger or unforgivable actions, harsh words or irreconcilable differences, that separated those fortunate enough to have loved and been loved in return. The two had no plans of separation, yet the icy hand of death stole their beloved from their arms and left them cold and empty. Does death take with it love?

I shook my head to push away the painful thoughts and unfolded the paper. My eyes scanned the page and saw all the crossed-out lines – the things we had accomplished.

Number one, *get married.* Number two, *have children.* Number four, *see the Geisha in Japan.* Number five, *travel through Italy.* Number twelve, *go on a road trip.* Number fourteen, *dive in the Great Barrier Reef.*

Our trip to Hawaii had been Evelyn's favourite. We went in 1974, when Evelyn was eleven. Number fifteen requested that we learnt to surf there. We were all only too willing to comply.

Christopher was fourteen and thought he knew everything. When he took to the surf for the first time, he was sorely disappointed to discover that everything didn't include surfing.

I spent most of the trip photographing the incredible land. There was an amazing mix of beach and forest and I couldn't get enough of it.

Grace wanted to hike up a volcano but, much to my relief, Christopher and Evelyn disagreed, much like they did on everything.

I had only told them about the list a month before we left. Our strange adventures around the world suddenly made sense to them. Evelyn had had nightmares for a solid week, about riots and blood and death, and Grace stayed in her room every night until she fell asleep.

I wasn't surprised about the nightmares - after all, I still had nightmares about that night – but it still hurt me to see her cry. I had gone into as little detail as possible, but Evelyn was incredibly intelligent, and she had figured out the details on her own.

I wondered if perhaps I shouldn't have said anything to her, but Grace was sure it was the right thing.

"The nightmares will settle down, Jack. It's important that they know why we do this. It's shaped our lives," she had said.

"Yeah," I mumbled, wishing I could take away Evelyn's fear. "I guess you're right."

The crinkle of the paper between my fingers brought me back to the moment. I had a plan. I looked down at number twenty-nine and smiled. *Learn to Ballroom Dance.*

I had already called a sitter.

I stood up from my chair and found Grace in the living room reading The Hobbit – again.

"Don't you ever get tired of that book?" I asked, knowing the answer already.

"Nope," she said, not taking her eyes from the page.

"I have a surprise for you," I said, with a mischievous grin on my face.

Grace looked up at me, delighted. "A surprise?"

"Yes. Go get changed. We're going out."

A wide smile spread across her face and she was out of her chair and running up the stairs.

Fifteen minutes later, we were out the door and into the nearest Taxi.

After dinner at her favourite restaurant, we hailed another Taxi and arrived at Georgia's Dance Studio.

"Number twenty-nine!" Grace said, excited. "I've wanted to do this for so long!"

"I know," I answered, gripping her hand and walking inside. "There's no time like the present."

Georgia, the instructor, prepared us for an evening of stepping on each other's feet and discovering our rhythm. Grace laughed more than she had in a long time and it made me feel so good to make her happy.

The waltz was her favourite.

"1, 2, 3. 1, 2, 3," she kept whispering to herself. It was a soft dance that made her smile. When the night was over, she begged to come back.

I promised we would.

Chapter Thirty-One

I sat in the stiff chair and watched as my little girl walked across the stage towards the rest of her life. How was it the end of 1981? How had the last eighteen years flown by so quickly? Wasn't it just the other day that she said her first word? Wasn't it just yesterday that I took her to her first day at school?

Grace sat beside me, her hands folded in her lap. I could tell she was trying to control herself. She was on the verge of tears. She looked so beautiful. She wore her hair down, with loose curls falling long past her shoulders. A few silver strands twirled amongst the chestnut waves. She wore no makeup and a black dress that stopped just past her knees.

"I can't believe that we're at our daughter's graduation. This is ridiculous," I whispered to her out of the corner of my mouth as the principal droned on.

"Do you remember Christopher's graduation?" she asked.

I cringed. I had cried like a baby. I had no intentions of reliving that experience. "How could I forget?"

I stood up to get a better view when they called the student I knew was just before Evelyn.

"Jack, sit down. The people behind you can't see," Grace hissed.

I didn't care. Not in the slightest. I swatted away her hand.

My youngest child, my beautiful Evelyn, was an adult. She was about to graduate. She was free to make decisions, move out, go to university, and start a family. For a moment, I felt redundant. My job was done, and I was no longer needed. Evelyn took after her mother as a capable and free spirit. Perhaps I had no place in her life anymore. I felt hot tears sting my eyes. I looked to the floor to gather myself.

"Evelyn Jane Leatherby."

I snapped my head up as the principal called her name and I saw my daughter smile at me. Evelyn's eyes shone, and her bright smile stretched across her lips. She held my gaze, winked at me, and stepped off stage.

No, I wasn't redundant. She still needed me. More than that, she still wanted her father. I clapped my hands so loudly that my palms were stinging and sobbed like a baby.

Again.

Grace and I waited for Evelyn by the school's fountain. The ceremony had been excruciatingly long, but that didn't bother me. We left the enormous school auditorium to discover it was an unusually freezing English day, with cold drizzle dampening my coat and sticking my hair to my neck. I tried to ignore the bitter wind and focus on the day.

"Gracie, can you believe we did it?" I asked.

"What do you mean?"

"Number three."

"What's number three?"

"*Raise a good family.* We raised two kids. Really well. Look at her!" I marveled at my daughter as she talked to her friends, hugging them goodbye. "You and I – I think we did a great job."

Gracie looked up and smiled at me. "Yeah, we did. Didn't we?"

I leant down and kissed her. I couldn't believe how much I still loved this woman. We had been married for twenty-three years and she was more to me now than she ever had been before.

"Gross!"

My lips parted from Grace's when Christopher wailed in distaste. Gracie laughed and shook her head and I stepped back sheepishly.

"Christopher," I said, "where were you? I couldn't find you during the ceremony. We had a seat saved."

"Oh, I told Mum I was sitting with Norah." Christopher grinned as he always did whenever his fiancé's name was mentioned. It was how I knew he truly loved her.

"Where is she?" I asked.

"She's gone to find her parents and tell them the amended date for the wedding."

"Amended date?" Grace asked.

"What do you mean?" I shoved my hands in my pockets, no longer able to feel my fingers.

"We're moving it forward." Christopher smiled and scrunched his shoulders. "We had no idea why we were waiting for so long."

I smiled. I remembered thinking something exactly like that once.

"The wedding is now in three months. On the twentieth."

My smile faded. I was about to become a father-in-law. My son was about to get married. Who knew how soon it would be before there were grandchildren. I was completely unprepared.

"That's great," I croaked. "Really. Excellent."

There had been far too many weddings in my life so far.

Christopher laughed, seeing the panicked expression on my face.

"Ah, there she is. The woman of the moment," Grace brushed past me and wrapped her arms around Evelyn's neck. "You did such a great job, honey. I love you so much."

"Thanks Mum," Evelyn replied, tightening her grip around her mother's waist. I could see tears in her eyes and hear fear in her voice.

When Grace let go, Christopher ruffled Evelyn's hair and insulted her. There is nothing quite like brotherly love.

Finally, it was my turn to congratulate my daughter. I pulled her close and kissed the top of her head.

"I'm scared, Daddy," she whispered into my ear.

"I know," I answered, squeezing my eyes closed to hold back the mutinous tears.

"Christopher, honey, why don't you take me to Norah? I want to talk some more about the details. The twentieth isn't exactly very far away."

I mentally thanked Grace for thinking of an excuse to take Christopher away.

Evelyn didn't let go of me. I heard quiet sobs and wished more than anything I could take away all of her fear. My heart was aching inside.

"This is it. I have to do it all alone, now. I don't know how."

"You don't have to do anything alone, Ev."

"Everything's going to be different. I'm so afraid."

I pulled back and took her face in my hands, squeezing her cheeks together like I used to when she was a little girl. "You don't have to be afraid of anything. It's going to be great. Just you wait and see. Soon you're going to wonder why you were so worried."

Evelyn chuckled and brushed my hands away. With the tip of my finger, I swept up a lone tear on her cheek and smiled. "See? You're going to be just fine."

"Thanks, Dad," she said.

"Go find your Mum. She'll be pestering Norah about everything. Save her from herself."

Evelyn laughed and nodded. I sucked in a deep, shocked breath as something in her face changed. In that moment, she grew up. She planted a steely resolve across her face and I knew she would be alright.

I had done what I could to prepare her for the world and, though I may not be redundant, Evelyn was right about one thing. Everything was going to be different.

Chapter Thirty-Two

Everything was different.

I missed my children. I missed hearing Chris and Evelyn fight over who got to watch what on the television. I missed afternoons with Chris, walking around Big Ben, and I missed the lack of silence when Evelyn was around.

Now that both of my children had moved out of home and I was far too rapidly approaching forty-five, I felt, almost, lost.

For the last twenty-four years, I had a purpose, a goal. I had to take care of my children, raise them well, see that they had everything they needed. Then all of a sudden, in one fell swoop, it was just Grace and me. Our house was our own again. Grace and I had helped Evelyn and Christopher pack and move their belongings and it was one of the hardest things I had ever had to do.

Grace was all smiles when the children were watching, but behind closed doors, when it was just her and me, the tears flowed freely. She didn't know what to do and I couldn't remember what it was like to live without them.

The halls were silent, the rooms empty. Suddenly I felt too small to be living in this house. I had been so afraid of being a father, but I had become accustomed to it, and now, without my son and my daughter in my house, I was afraid of just being me again.

Life is a constant, ever changing river and I often found it difficult to follow the stream. It seemed that at just the moment you were comfortable, life turned around and threw you upside down until you couldn't see where you were going. Days ticked by and you had to discover how to adjust to the new order, the new pattern. Then, when that began to make sense, the world shifted again until you could no longer tell which way was up.

It was just a few days ago that I had sat in an old, uncomfortable pew and watched my son get married. What was happening to the world? How could I be the father of a married man?

Norah looked lovely, as all brides do on their wedding day, and Chris looked more nervous than I had anticipated. I gave him the one piece of advice I could as I helped him get ready that morning.

"Make sure she's the right one, Chris," I said, putting my hands on his shoulders. "The Leatherby men fall in love once and only once."

"What do you mean?" he asked.

"My father used to tell me that the men in the Leatherby family only ever loved one woman. Even if she dies, he remains faithful til the end. It's once and once only. So, you have to make it count."

As the preacher spoke and the ceremony passed, I felt something strange inside me. I could tangibly feel time slipping away, disappearing as palpably as sand running through my fingers.

I felt the world stir, twisting and cracking, until I felt I was standing on the edge of a precipice, overlooking a canyon as deep and as unmoving as the earth's core. It was my life, an inconsequential, hollow pit in the middle of the inescapable conundrum of reality.

Everyone carried on about their own business, unconcerned by the fact that the world doesn't actually make any sense. People pursue the right jobs, enough money, security and material belongings, but in the enormous sense of it all, none of that mattered.

Life mattered. The very essence of life, the act of truly living, of taking from each day everything you can and giving back in abundance.

The congregation clapped and stood to their feet as loud music swelled, pulling me back from the brink of my world and into the moment that my son walked down the aisle with his wife.

That night, when the reception was over, and the night had grown old, I wandered the empty halls of my home and felt the thick stillness in the air. I touched the walls, hoping they still carried the voices of the lives that had been lived here.

In my mind's eye, I saw birthdays, Christmases, and irreplaceable moments pass. I saw Evelyn aged seven, running down the hall; Christopher aged fifteen, chasing his sister around the living room; Grace aged twenty-three, tracing her fingers along her stomach, awaiting the arrival of her unborn child.

I stopped in the middle of the hall and leant against the cool wall. I slid down until I was on the floor and rested my head back against the cool surface. I could hardly breathe. I pulled my knees close to me and drowned in the silence.

I decided a trip was in order. My pictures were selling well, and the list was not yet complete. We needed to get away, to get a fresh perspective, and rediscover ourselves together.

Twelve days after Christopher had married his high school sweetheart, and nine days after Grace had left to see the world on her own, the silence was too much to take. We left for Thailand.

We should have researched the climate before we left. It was unfathomably hot, especially when we had just left a bitterly cold winter. Sticky and rainy, with thunderstorms and air so thick you could hardly breathe, I wondered why I picked Thailand. Despite the heat, the country was often beautiful, and it was in Chiang Mi that we were able to cross off number eighteen.

Truthfully, I was afraid. I was in a country I didn't know, listening to people who couldn't speak my language and was about to ride atop an elephant. Grace was ecstatic. She had always wanted to do this. I, however, had never had the desire to be high up in the air on an unpredictable animal that could trample me into nothing underfoot.

Nevertheless, when I was up there, I saw the world from a completely different perspective and before I knew it, I relaxed - I was having fun.

I supposed that the only thing that made the twists and turns of life bearable, were the sweet moments that popped up out of nowhere. These were the moments that never shouted at you or demanded their presence be made known. These were the moments that put life in its place and staved off the pain and the confusion for want of a second of joy.

During that moment, when I sat on top of an elephant in Thailand, a million miles from home, I forgot I felt lost. I felt a small piece of me coming back. For just a moment, I felt peace. I felt young again.

I was in a hurry. It was Grace's birthday and her gift had only arrived an hour ago, which meant I had to go and collect it.

I drove along the road with Grace's gift on the passenger's seat. I wanted to give her something special this year, something important. I hoped I had managed. It was a book and I wanted her to get it as soon as possible.

The lorry came from out of nowhere. In the fraction of a second my mind had to consider the reasons behind my inescapable death, I supposed that the driver had run a red light. A common occurrence, a random moment in time that would bring me to my knees and shatter my life.

I had just enough time, before the truck ran into the side of my car, to wish I had just a little more time. I was only fifty-three - old to someone still cloaked in the armor of youth, yet not old enough.

I was thrust to the side and I felt my head slap against the window. My vision began to falter, blurring in and out like a television with a faulty aerial. My stomach rolled around like an angry sea as the car flipped in the air, rotating twice before crashing down onto the road. The car thudded with the force but continued to roll like dice thrown with too much force.

Finally, there was relief. The car stopped moving. I felt blood rush to my pounding head and my eyes filled with a thick substance, tainting the world with an inky crimson. I could feel pain from somewhere, but my mind couldn't find the location. My hands dropped against the roof and it was then that I realised I was upside down, trapped by my seatbelt.

I couldn't hold on to consciousness any longer. My eyelids fluttered, and as my eyes absorbed blood, they began to sting. I felt so weak. I couldn't find the strength to lift the eyelids that now seemed to weigh more than the earth. I let my eyes stay closed, surrendering to the pain.

Blackness came, and the world was gone.

I was here. I couldn't touch. I couldn't taste or feel, but I was still here. I knew I wasn't gone yet. I was holding on. How? Why?

The pain was too intense, too great for me to handle. My body was ailing, but my mind fought on. I wanted to give in. There was acid in every vein, fire in every bone. I begged my mind to let my body surrender. Death was the acceptable tax paid by those fortunate enough to have taken that first breath, and I wanted to pay. I couldn't handle the agony.

Suddenly my heart began to slow. *Ba-boom....ba-boom.* I was getting my wish. It was finally coming to an end. I felt as though my limbs no longer belonged to me. My mind was prying itself away from my body, detangling itself from the attachment to the shell I would leave behind. The pain eased. I was about to die. I was about to escape into sweet, blessed relief.

All I could see was black fog, echoing out in front of me in a timeless marshland. There was nothing and everything in the emptiness of it all. Every moment I spent on earth poured into the quicksand of the end until it became lost and blurred in the numbing pain that ravaged every cell of my body.

I wasn't afraid. The moments were not pointless. The moments were what had made up my time, the time that was now over. They mattered, each and every second. The days of peace, the moments of joy, the droplets of love, cascading in front of me and disappearing into the finale, gave point and purpose to the fifty-three years I had spent here. Perhaps the world would have been different if I had not been in it, and I wondered how it would grow and change and improve when I wasn't there to see it.

As I stared across at the hollowness of the black fog, I realised it didn't feel the way I thought it would. There was no finality to the end, no burning desire to have done it all again.

There was simply the knowledge that my time was done. I knew I had been the best Jack Leatherby I could. I did my best to live each day with strength and determination and joy. I had soldiered on through a life that could have been the death of me, to get as much as I could and give even more.

I wondered what would happen when my heart pounded its very last beat. I didn't know. I didn't know the protocol for death. There was, however, one thing I felt certain of – the blackness would not last.

Something else would come.

I was ready. I had lived and loved and fought and surrendered and experienced everything I could in the time that had been allotted to me. I felt peace as the pictures of my past continued to disappear.

As I watched it all slipping away, something stabbed my heart. Hot lava poured through the most important muscle in my body, tracing through every pump and aorta. I wanted to scream. My heart began to pick up speed; something was dragging me back from the cusp of eternity.

No! I shouted voicelessly. My words were silenced by the darkness, taken into the blackness and buried amidst the fog. *Let me go!*

No one could hear me. I couldn't remember how to make a sound.

Chapter Thirty-Three

The pain increased, and I watched as the black fog lethargically began to recede. My heart was racing. Too fast. It hurt, ached, stung. The only thing I could feel was pain.

I was lost in the murky waters between alive and dead, earth and eternity, and I was drowning. Muffled voices filled my ears, but I couldn't make out the words they spoke. I didn't care.

I felt something as cold as ice yet as hot as fire trace through my arm and I suffered from its effects immediately. I was losing myself, but I fought to keep hold, until I could fight no longer, and I couldn't feel anything at all.

"Sir?"

My mind stirred into the forefront. Had someone spoken?

"Sir, can you hear me?"

Someone was out there. Someone was talking to me. But how could I get to them? I searched, looking for the way to open my eyes.

"Sir?"

"Leave it, Finch. I don't think he's ready to come around yet."

Wait, I tried to say. *I'm here.*

"I thought I saw him move, though, Doctor Landon."

"They do that sometimes. Doesn't mean anything."

"But look doctor. He moved again."

I had done it. Moving my hand was a small feat, but it meant I was one step closer to opening my eyes.

I heard a man sigh and then I felt cold fingers on my wrist. My heartbeat pounded against his fingers.

Suddenly I could see a man hovering over me. I had managed to open my eyes. I wanted to cry with relief. I could see again. Gone was the black fog, the empty fullness of the dark.

"See, doctor?" someone said.

"Hello, sir," said the man staring intently into my eyes. "Welcome back. Do you know where you are?"

I tried to speak, but all that came out was a rusty croak.

"Here," said the other voice. "Drink this."

A cup was held under my lips and I could see the man attached to the voice. He was young, with black hair and brown eyes. He titled the cup, so I could drink. I felt the cool liquid coat the back of my throat, drenching the desert.

"That's enough, Finch." The cup disappeared. "Let's try that again now, shall we sir? Do you know where you are?"

"H-hos..." I cleared my throat and coughed. "H-hospital?" I guessed, seeing the badge on his coat that read 'Dr. Eric Landon.'

"Yes, very good."

"Do you remember anything that happened?" The young man named Finch peered forwards.

"Uh." I tried to clear the cloudiness from my brain, to make sense of what was going on. All I could remember was a phone call about Grace's gift and foggy black marshlands. The space in between was vacant. "N-no."

"Alright," said Doctor Landon. "You were in a car accident. Your car was hit by a lorry."

My stomach lurched.

"You have suffered some very serious injuries, but, you are now out of harm's way. The worst is over."

I tried to nod.

"Do you remember your name?" Doctor Landon asked.

"Jack," I said, without hesitation.

"Is there someone we can call for you, Jack? You were found without any identification. What's your last name?"

"What do you mean? How long have I been out?" I asked. How long had I been here without Grace knowing where I was?

"You've been here for six days so far, sir," Finch said weakly.

"What?" I said, shaking. "Grace! Gracie!" I began to shout her name, over and over again, feeling gut-wrenching fear in my stomach. Where was she? Did she fear the worst?

"Sir, calm down!" the doctor was shouting, leaning forward to restrain me. I tried to move, ripping out the drip inserted into my arm. I felt the little tube tear out of my skin.

"Grace! Grace!" I continued to shriek, fighting against the doctor and immeasurable pain as I tried to get out of the bed and back to my Grace.

"Jack, calm down," Finch was saying softly, as he put his hand on my shoulder.

I swatted his hand off and shouted out, desperate to be free.

"Give me the sedative!" Landon shouted, forcing my arms down.

Finch hesitated.

"Now!" Landon screeched.

Finch turned around and opened a drawer, pulling out a large syringe.

"Now, Finch!" Landon yelled.

My heart raced inside my chest and I lost all control. I screamed and tried to shake free of Landon's grasp. I couldn't see past the panic attack causing me to spiral into an anxious seizure.

Finch stabbed me with the needle and purged the contents into my bloodstream. "It's alright," he said softly. "It's going to be alright. Calm down."

My body went limp and my eyes fluttered wildly. I fell back against the bed and into oblivion.

Chapter Thirty-Four

It was dark when I woke up. The clock on the far wall said three seventeen. The room was painted with silver, giving a ghostly illumination to every object in the room. From underneath the closed door I saw a stream of yellow light and if I concentrated, I could hear the voices of nurses, chatting and encouraging each other through the long graveyard shift.

In the far corner of the room used to be a chair. I noticed its absence and looked around, only to find it closer to my bed and containing a crumpled figure.

"Grace?" I said in a raspy voice.

The figure stirred and looked at me through the darkness. "Jack!" Grace sat forward and took my hand in hers. "Jack, are you alright? I was searching everywhere for you. I called all the hospitals."

"I'm fine," I said, my voice cracking with the lump in my throat. I squeezed her fingers tightly.

"I thought I'd lost you," she said. I could hear her quiet sobs.

"Come here." I pulled her hand forward until she was leaning across the bed, her head on my chest. "I'm still here."

"I was so scared," she whimpered, drenching the blanket with her tears.

"I'm so sorry, Gracie," I said, running my fingers through her hair.

"It's been two weeks." She sniffed and sat back, pressing her palm against my cheek.

I let out a deep sigh. The last thing I remembered was waking up six days after the accident. I must have been asleep since then.

"I didn't know. I've been asleep."

"Your body needs rest," Grace said, leaning forward and kissing my forehead.

"Did they say what was wrong with me?" I asked, feeling every ache and pain in my body as if it were fresh.

"No, but you look terrible."

I smiled and traced the line of her jaw. "You should go home, Gracie," I whispered.

"What? No!" She looked appalled.

"Gracie, look at the time. I'm surprised they haven't kicked you out already."

"Well, I hid in the bathroom. I wasn't going to leave you."

I breathed out a laugh. "Thank you. It's so good to see you. I've missed you more than you know."

"You've been asleep."

"I still miss you in my sleep." I held her stare for what felt like forever.

Grace pulled my hand from her face and kissed my palm. "I don't want to go."

"I know. But if you don't go, and they find you, you'll get in trouble and they might not let you back or something."

"I'm sure they wouldn't do that."

"Grace, it's three thirty in the morning. Go home. Get some sleep. I love you. Come back tomorrow. It's okay."

"Really?" she asked, skeptical.

"Really. Sleep."

"Alright," she conceded, kissing my palm once more and then laying it down beside me. "You rest. I'll be back tomorrow as soon as the stupid visiting hours say I can, okay?"

"Okay."

Grace headed for the door and paused. "I'm just a phone call away."

"I know."

Grace peered out and waited for the moment she could leave the room without being noticed. As the door closed behind her, I felt sick, empty, and weak. I wanted her to stay, but she looked so tired, so frightened. It was best if she went home and took care of herself.

I turned my head and stared at the window, wishing I was a more selfish man.

My eyes opened, snapping me out of my dreams. Sunlight was filling the room.

"Ah, Mr. Leatherby!" Doctor Landon walked into the room and smiled. "Are you feeling better?"

"Yes. Thank you," I said, feeling uncomfortable around Landon.

"Now, is there anyone I can call for you? Your wife maybe?" he asked, looking over a thick file.

"No," I said. "It's okay. She found me. She saw me last night."

"Oh," Landon said, looking up, surprised. "Okay. That's excellent."

I nodded, unsure what to say.

"I have good news for you. As long as nothing terrible happens within the next twenty-four hours, I'm satisfied enough with your improvements to send you home."

"Really?" I asked.

"Yes sir. You've been making excellent progress. Your leg is well and truly on its way to being healed and the ribs shouldn't be too much of a problem for you, either. I'm glad you've gotten plenty of sleep."

"I don't remember anything since you sedated me," I said.

"Don't worry. That's perfectly normal. You'll regain your memories very soon."

"Have I woken up?"

"Oh, yes. Quite a few times. That's how I finally learned your last name. You called out for Grace a lot. Is she your wife?"

"Y-yes," I said, wondering why I couldn't remember waking up.

"Jack," Landon began, seeing the worry on my face. "There is nothing to worry about. I promise. The body needs sleep to recuperate and you did have a nasty hit to your head. I'd be surprised if your memory wasn't a little foggy. Really. It's okay. You're healing very well."

"What happened to me in the accident?"

Landon put the folder he was holding down and looked up as if in thought. "Well, your left leg is broken. It's healing well, but we did have to operate, and you will, unfortunately, likely walk with a limp from now on. You cracked a few ribs - all of which are healing very nicely - had a severe concussion, a myocardial infarction, and you have also accumulated a rather impressive number of cuts and contusions."

"A h-heart attack?"

"Yes. When you were on the table, you did suffer a heart attack after your heart nearly stopped all together. I hadn't ever seen a reaction quite like that."

"What?"

187

"Jack, please, it's all alright. I promise. It was just a minor heart attack, you are perfectly fine. When you go home, though, you must be on bed rest. Is that understood?"

"Yes," I answered, just happy to be allowed to go home. "I understand."

"Excellent."

Landon left the room and I looked down at my leg. It was covered in plaster and elevated. I looked at my arms and saw purple and yellow blushes of healing bruises. I lifted a hand to my head, where there was a bump that was just about flat again.

I had come so close to dying, so close to leaving the world behind. I sighed and leant back against the pillow, letting myself drift back to sleep.

Chapter Thirty-Five

It was 1995, and the accident that had very nearly claimed my life was just four years ago. I was allowed to go home those twenty-four hours later and recovering was a slow, painful, and lonely process.

I was given both a wheelchair and crutches to use to help me to get around when it was necessary. I hated the idea of being bound to a chair, unable to freely move as I wished.

The cast ran from my toes to my hip. It was awkward, big, and uncomfortable. I couldn't sleep more than two hours at a time.

When the cast had come off, I had hoped that soon after I would be walking normally again, that the doctor's prognosis had been wrong.

It wasn't.

Every step I took was marred with a limp.

I refused to be someone who made everyone else's life miserable during the recovery time. I was as positive and as self-sufficient as I could manage.

When I became overwhelmed, I withdrew to my bedroom and sat by myself in silence, gaining the courage and the strength to grit my teeth and bare it.

Finally, I felt I was ready to live again. I had bided my time, healing, recovering – both mentally and physically – and taking everything as slowly as possible.

This was to be my first trip since the accident.

I had put the list on the mantelpiece above the fireplace and left it to gather dust while I fought to keep a hold of life's joy. My body was ageing, so healing was so much slower than I remembered. I was determined to see it through, never to lose heart or faith.

When I had decided enough was enough, I slowly walked to the mantelpiece, accustomed to the limp in my leg, and pulled down the list. I held it in my hands and blew away the dust. Unfolding it gently, I heard the familiar crunch of the browned paper that had been mine for thirty-six years.

My eyes scanned the paper - the words that had been crossed off, the things yet to be accomplished.

Where would Grace and I travel to this time? We had been to Hawaii, Japan, China, Italy, France, Thailand, Germany, Australia and we had seen so many incredible things already. What could we do that would light our hearts on fire again?

Number twenty-four was to walk along the Hollywood Boulevard, number thirty was to spend a week exploring New York City and number thirty-seven was to see Elvis in concert.

I decided to do them all. Since we couldn't see Elvis in concert, I figured a visit to Graceland was the next best thing. I called my travel agent and she organized the entire trip.

A month later, we were gone.

We decided Hollywood Boulevard was the first stop. Grace and I walked down the pathway, stepping on stars filled with the names of celebrities, looking out at the surreal world we had found ourselves in.

From Hollywood, we left for New York, where we saw Broadway shows – Grace's favourite being *Gentlemen Prefer Blondes* - ate at fine restaurants and wandered around the massive buildings. It was a grey, concrete world, yet there was something intriguing about it. Everyone seemed to be in such a hurry to get where they were going, and I wondered what it must be like to live your life always late for somewhere else. Did they ever see what was right in front of them?

Memphis, Tennessee was an incredible place. Elvis Presley was everywhere and visiting Graceland was a dreamlike experience. It was as though time had frozen and overlooked this place, left it alone to preserve the memory of someone who had passed long ago.

Since August 1977, the second storey of Graceland had been off limits – not even employees of Graceland were allowed to see it. Only Lisa Marie and Priscilla were allowed up there. We walked past two security officers guarding the stairs as we wandered around and I found myself appreciating their presence.

For someone so deep in the public eye, it was right that some things remained private, even after his death. I couldn't imagine living my life under scrutiny, the way Elvis had. To have every move you may or may not have made documented as though it were vital information the world relied on, could have blurred the lines between reality and fiction.

I was glad there were some things that, no matter the pressure from the world, remained untouched.

"Don't tell me what to do!" Grace yelled at me in our hotel room.

"I'm not! You're so sensitive!" I wasn't even sure what we were fighting about anymore.

"Please! Just save it. Ever since the accident, you've moped around as if the world owes you some sort of apology!" Grace crossed her arms and turned to face the window.

Nothing had changed in the years that we had been married. She was still as fiery as ever. Truthfully, I loved it about her.

Most of the time.

"Oh, I'm so sorry that my car accident has been hard on you!"

"Don't give me that pity party rubbish, Jack! You know what I mean."

"Yeah, I do. You mean that everything is about you." I paced back and forth angrily.

"That's not even close to the truth, Jack! You're a stubborn, pig-headed man who is angry that his leg hurts! Get over it."

I was silent. I didn't have a rebuttal for the painful words she shouted at me.

"You have to learn to live again, Jack! Look where we are! We're in Memphis! This used to excite you! Where has that gone?"

"It still does," I said quietly.

"Then why do you walk around like you're so miserable all the time?" Grace turned to face me again, her back to the window.

"I don't know! I'm sorry! Would you just stop screaming at me, you entitled little princess!" I shouted.

"Yeah, I would stop shouting if you weren't such a-"

I cut her off, pressing my lips against hers. Her lips softened under mine and the argument was over. We fought, but we were closer than ever. I loved her more than words could say.

Chapter Thirty-Six

I held my grandson in my arms, remembering the days of old. I stood in the living room, watching my family live around me. They laughed and smiled, and I wished I could freeze this moment. I wished I could make it all last forever. I took a mental photograph and knew that it would remain there forever, fixed in the hard drive of my brain. There it would be safe from the weather and old age, and cracks and time.

Christopher laughed, and I looked up to see him kiss Grace on the cheek. His wife, Norah, was cutting up carrots and Evelyn was laughing, lost in a world of her own, the world she had shown me through her kindness, young heart, and joyful spirit.

I was proud of them, proud of the people they had become. My son was married with four children, the youngest of whom was six months old, and my daughter was married and enjoying a successful career. Grace was still in love with me and I was still alive. My brother was happily married with three children of his own, and though my father had passed, we had established a relationship before the end.

I held no ill feelings or moments of regret. Everything that had happened in our relationship had formed us both into the men we were. He had given up alcohol and was back running the garage. His relationship with Frankie had been repaired until the memories of bitterness had faded like an old dream.

As the years trickled past, we had followed along the line of time, making the most of every moment. Gradually, we grew closer to finishing the list that had changed our lives.

I often wondered where we would be without it. It had given us the chance to experience life, just as Grace had always wished. That had been my aim, all those many years ago when I had fallen in love with a woman who changed the colour of my sky. I wanted to show her everything the world had to offer.

I kissed the forehead of my grandson, Harley Jack Leatherby, and passed him back to Christopher. My children left the house after one of our regular Sunday lunches and Grace and I stood on the porch, watching as they got into their Taxis and disappeared into the heavy pour of rain.

I gripped Grace's hand in mine and felt the warmth of her frail skin. It was nice just to hold her hand. Even after all these years, she still cried when our children left. I loved her for that. I pulled her close to me, swaying to the sound of the rain.

We barely moved our feet. I remembered doing this so many years ago. Outside of her house, in the pouring rain, we waltzed under the streetlights without even moving. Just two kids, wishing for a future, a hope and a love that would last the ages.

Our youth was gone now. We were old. There was no escaping the truth. I was seventy-one, and living each day to the fullest took its toll. My skin was wrinkled, and my eyes were growing dim. I had always hoped that when I was old, I would still stand tall, see clearly and move about without hindrance. I had seen men older than me who lived as though they were only fifty years old. I wished that could be me.

But it wasn't and that was alright. I could hardly believe the life we had lived. Out of all of the things we had accomplished and the places we had been, I knew it was the small, seemingly insignificant moments that I treasured the most. The sun breaking through the grey clouds after days of London's drizzle, Grace's smile, my children's laughter. I would have traded it all - every dollar I ever had, every possession I ever owned - I would have given it all for those moments.

I twirled Grace around and she laughed, her eyes lighting up and her face glowing with exuberance and hope. She wrapped her arm around my waist and we sat down on the porch swing beside the door, protected from the rain and the cold wind.

This time, after our dance in the rain, I didn't have to walk away from her. I got to stay. We sat in front of the house we had shared our lives in and looked over the memories of a life well lived. As we sat together, I reached into my coat pocket and pulled out a browned piece of paper - paper that had my heart, our lives, etched into every fiber, hidden inside every ink splotched word.

It was the list that had helped to write the story of our lives during our short, humble time here on earth.

Grace leaned into my side as I took my round glasses from my other pocket and slipped them on. Slowly, I opened the folded paper and cleared my throat.

"So," I began, "where should we go to next?"

Chapter Thirty-Seven

My back was pressed against the cool grass, and the sun was beginning to descend on the horizon. The orange sky would soon fade to dusty pink before it melted away into a sea of endless black. I could already see the shadow of the moon in the sky and one lone star hanging far above my head like a glimmering doorway to another world. I looked across at my Gracie and smiled softly. I hoped that she had enjoyed her birthday, just sitting with me, reminiscing.

I noticed the small, rectangular gift that I had for her, still sat unopened. I lifted myself up and reached for it. It felt heavy in my frail hands, but I knew its weight would be almost insignificant to a younger man.

"Let me open it for you, my darling," I said, tinkering with the golden ribbon. "That is if I can ever get into it," I added under my breath with a faint chuckle.

Finally, I was able to remove the pesky bow. I flung it away and watched it drop to the ground from the corner of my eye. I set to work on the wrapping, carefully lifting the bits of tape so as not to tear the paper. Gracie hated for the paper to be torn.

"Almost there," I breathed, sighing at how long it took me to open the gift.

I lifted the last tab and pulled away the paper to reveal a hardcover book. I smiled and held it up for her to see. I hoped she would like it.

On the front cover of the book was the photo of her that I had taken when we were at the beach so many years ago. The same photo I had given her for her eighteenth birthday. She looked so beautiful, so peaceful. She was in the middle of a graceful spin, her hair floating in the forceful breeze, just as a lightning strike smacked the ocean behind her.

"This is my favourite photo of you," I said, setting the book down in front of her. "I thought the picture was appropriate for the title. I've called it *Rope the Wind*. In this one, we travel to Ireland. It's the last thing on that list I made for us."

I stole another look at the book I had written, before I gazed back to my Gracie. Her name was carved deeply into the rounded stone that stretched up to form an angel looking down, sorrow lined on its smooth features. Etched just below her name were the words,

Adored wife who changed the colour of a man's sky.

A dried leaf floated along the breeze and landed on the top of her headstone. My brows furrowed, and I leant forward to brush it off.

I kept my eyes on her, seeing her beautiful face in my mind, undisturbed by the hand of time. I pressed my hands against the cool stone and traced my fingers along the contours of her name. My heart ached as it always did - an ever-present twist of pain that continually shocked me with its violence. I loved her just as much as I did on the day we said, "I do." I had been right, all those years ago – I would never love again. How could I, when my heart had always, and would always, belong to her?

"I know you hate presents, but the timing was perfect. The release date coincided with your birthday. Gracie, I think it's...maybe even better than the others." My voice shook with ageless agony, as I brushed my crooked fingers through what was left of my hair. For her, I would contain my pain until I went home, leaving her here for the night, in this hateful cemetery, as I always did. How I despised doing it. But I would be back tomorrow and then I would plaster a brave face, yet again, over my wrinkled and spotted skin.

That way, she wouldn't ever have to know how horrifically the throbbing wound caused by her absence slaughtered me every day.

More than two years had passed since I first touched pen to paper to write the story found in *Rope the Wind*. It was considerably longer than the others. Somehow, I felt a stronger connection to it. I wasn't sure that that was even possible. Perhaps it was because it was the very last item on the list.

For so many years, I had tried to contain life. I had tried to hold onto it, gripping tightly at the fraying edges of time, in a pointless attempt to stop it from vanishing. But life has a funny way of surprising you. Somehow, it tore its way free of my grasp and took the life I cared most for and held onto with the most ferocity. *Hers.*

In one moment, our future was stolen. What could have been was taken, never to be returned. All it took was one unrelenting stroke of illness and she was gone, her life erased. I remembered holding her lifeless hand in the early morning in our London home, unprepared for the tragedy, unequipped with the strength to handle the torturous grief.

Trying to hold onto her life had been like trying to rope the wind. No matter your strength, the wind cannot be tamed. Akin to life, it remains elusive, untouched and undamaged by our pathetic and weak attempts to control the ever flowing current.

I had beaten myself, searching for answers. Where was the justice in her death? Why do some live, when others die? How can a life be snuffed out like a candle in a pointless breeze? Why had I been forced to continue living, day to day, with a pain that was incomprehensibly not quite strong enough to kill me, when she lay motionless under the heavy, cool earth?

I had never found the answers. But then, could anyone?

I was afraid, so very afraid. I found myself very suddenly alone – more alone than I had ever been. She was gone, and she was never coming back. I shook with an unchanging fear while the irreplaceable light in my life was darkened by the black hand of death.

I reached around to my satchel and opened it. I pulled out handful after handful of books, laying them out beside the newest addition. My heart was heavy in my chest, my breathing labored. I traced the tips of my shaking fingers along their covers, seeing my Gracie's face reflected back at me in seventeen different ways. Seventeen photos I had taken of her while she still lived.

"I'm so sorry it had to be this way," I whispered, hot tears threatening to spill down my face.

Books filled with the story of our life together was the only gift I could give to her - our time in Cuba, meeting Catalina and Joaquin, gondolas in Italy, diving in Australia, Graceland in Memphis, the Geisha in Japan, riding elephants in Thailand.

It was the life she had wanted. The life she had been deprived of.

The life I wrote for her.

I missed her more than any words to any story could say. My mind clung to the moment I dreamed of her in the hospital after my car accident. The sweetest dream, the softest moment. She was there. She was right beside me, drenching my chest with her tears. But when the morning light came, I was alone. It was the closest I had come to touching her in far more years than I could bear to imagine.

I had come so close to joining her, so close to leaving the world behind, but my heart had held our time at ransom by keeping its steady beat.

I picked up the latest journey I had created for her and cleared my throat, begging the emotion that laced my voice to vanish. I opened the book and began to read a story from our life together, the life we had never had.

Grace had wanted to live, and I had found a way that she could, even after her life was taken. I died inside when Grace closed her eyes for the last time.

Joaquin's list was mine, a figment of my imagination.

A dead man's list for a life unlived.

A paper heart.

I looked up at her every so often and smiled, reliving the life that never was, as the words flowed freely from my lips. My mind's eye formed my wife's face in all its glory and I was lost in the life I wished so desperately that I had lived off paper. I missed the children I had never had, the moments I had never lived. I was drowning in the chocolate brown of her eyes, believing that we had truly travelled to Ireland and that I had, even if only for the briefest moment, been able to rope the wind.

My eyes grew foggy and dim and my chest began to hurt. I closed the book and shuffled closer to her. I felt it coming. It was only right that it should happen here, only right that she should hold my hand when it happened, as I had held hers. I lay back down beside her, unable to keep my body up any longer.

I wasn't afraid. I had everything to gain and nothing to lose. I had already lost the only thing that mattered, and now it was time for me to get it back. My chest was tightening, clenching like a balled-up fist. It wouldn't be long now. I pictured the family I never had, saying a soft farewell, as my heart beat its last, ignoring the words etched into the tombstone that, if read, would have contradicted the stories I had made for us.

Grace Leatherby

Adored Wife Who Changed the Colour of a Man's Sky

April 9th, 1940 – June 18th, 1958

Part of every misery is, so to speak, the misery's shadow or reflection:
the fact that you don't merely suffer but have to keep on thinking
about the fact that you suffer. I not only live each endless day in grief,
but live each day thinking about living each day in grief.

C. S. Lewis